CHAPTER ONE

BLAKE STOOD NEXT to the groom, wondering what the hell he was doing, being best man at this wedding. He knew this marriage wouldn't last—knew it was just a matter of time.

He'd tried to reason with Lachlan. But nothing could dissuade him. Not even Blake's argument that he himself had married at the same age—twenty-four—and the marriage hadn't lasted six months.

At least the bride wasn't an actress, Blake reasoned more positively. Also on the plus side, it wasn't as though marriage—even a temporary one—harmed a movie star's popularity these days. Gone were the days when the powerbrokers of Hollywood had dictated who a star could marry. *And* when.

The rise of social media had changed all that. The public couldn't get enough of celebrity relationships. They especially enjoyed break-ups and divorces, and any whiff of scandal. Such was life in the spotlight.

Thankfully Blake's own life wasn't so much in the spotlight—though he'd gained a little more attention in the press since moving Fantasy Productions from Sydney to LA fifteen months ago. Still, movie-makers—even very successful, very wealthy ones like himself—didn't grab the headlines the way actors did. Especially those like Lachlan, with his golden boy looks, buffed body and bedroom blue eyes. Add to that buckets of boyish charm and you had a prize publicity package.

Blake had first recognised Lachlan's potential when he'd attended a performance at Australia's much lauded National Institute of Dramatic Art a few years ago. He'd instantly signed him up. And the rest, as they said, was history. Three years and four movies later Lachlan was an established star, whilst *he'd* become Australia's most successful film writer/director/producer.

Blake suspected, however, that their working relationship would not last for much longer. It was only a matter of time before something—like this marriage—would make his star move on.

'There she is,' Lachlan whispered suddenly, snapping Blake out of his cynical thoughts.

Blake followed the groom's enthralled gaze past the seated guests and up the sweeping staircase down which the bride would eventually descend, and into the large living area, which had been filled with several rows of chairs divided by a strip of red carpet.

Blake spied a froth of white up on the gallery landing. White dress, white hair, white flowers. Behind the bride, attending to the long white veil, bustled the one and only bridesmaid, wearing something long and svelte in jade-green. Blake couldn't see her properly—didn't have a clue who she was. He hadn't even met the bride, having been too busy with his latest movie, plus several other new projects, to fly back to Australia for Lachlan's engagement party, and only jetting in to Sydney late last night.

The only contribution Blake had made to this wedding had been getting billionaire Byron Maddox—who was a good friend as well as a business partner—to offer his very lovely harbour-side home as a venue for the wedding and the reception afterwards.

The original venue had rather inconveniently burnt down six weeks ago, throwing Lachlan into a panic after getting a phone call on location from his hysterical bride-to-be.

Thank heaven for rich friends, Blake thought, and threw Byron and Cleo a grateful glance.

When they smiled back at him his own face cracked open into a wide smile. God, but they were a great couple. If ever a man and woman were made for each other it was those two. They almost made him believe in true love.

Finally some music started up. Not a traditional bridal march but a rather romantic piano rendition of 'The First Time Ever I Saw Your Face'.

It was at that moment that the bridesmaid in jade-green moved round from behind the Barbie doll bride and came into full view.

Blake's dark eyebrows lifted in surprise. She wasn't a stunner. But she was extremely attractive. Tall, with a slender figure and pale skin which suited the off-the-shoulder style of her gown. Her hair was a golden-brown colour, drawn straight back from her high forehead and falling in a softly waved curtain down her back, held in place by a simple circlet of pink and white flowers. It was her face, however, which Blake kept returning to—a face any camera would love.

Blake had a habit of looking at faces as though through a lens, especially on a first meeting. It was a long-ingrained habit, and one which didn't do any harm, really. No one knew what he was thinking at the time, so Blake didn't feel any guilt as he continued to assess the bridesmaid's looks from every camera angle.

He knew from experience that high cheekbones and a well-defined jawline photographed well in any light and from any angle. This woman's nose wasn't starlet-small, but it suited her, giving her face character. She didn't have pouting bee-stung lips either, although it was all the fad these days. Her mouth was actually rather wide, but still well formed. And expressive. So were her almond-shaped eyes.

Blake frowned as he tried to fathom the reason behind the sadness he kept glimpsing within their dark brown depths as she made her way slowly—and stiffly—down the staircase. Along with the sadness lay undeniable tension, he noted. Her knuckles were white as she clasped the posy of pink and white flowers at her waist with unnecessary force.

At last she reached the bottom step. It was at this point that she sucked in a deep breath, as though trying to gather all her courage. The gesture touched him, evoking an uncharacteristic surge of compassion. Something was bothering that girl about this wedding—something much more emotional and personal than Blake's cynical view.

'Who's the bridesmaid?' Blake muttered under his breath, so that only Lachlan could hear.

'What? Oh, that's Kate. Maddie's sister.'

'Older sister?'

'Older? Yeah. God, doesn't Maddie look incredible?' he exclaimed, clearly awed by the beauty of his bride, who remained standing at the top of the staircase, all eyes on her.

Not Blake's, however. He'd had his fill of Barbie doll blondes—especially those manufactured in Hollywood by plastic surgeons and ambitious mamas. His eyes were all for the bridesmaid, with her natural-looking figure and lovely but oh, so sad eyes.

Her chin lifted as she took her first step along

the makeshift aisle, her focus straight ahead during what seemed to be a very difficult journey for her. She didn't look at him, or at Lachlan, or at any of the guests. She seemed frozen now—a robot with no feelings on show any more. But that didn't mean they weren't there.

Smile, sweetheart, came the sudden wish from deep inside Blake. *Don't let the world see that you're hurting. Don't give people the chance to hurt you further.*

And they would if she let them. People could be cruel—especially once they'd sensed weakness. Fortunately, no one was looking at her. All eyes were still on the beaming bride, who was now approaching the bottom of the staircase. The music changed to 'Isn't She Beautiful?' Which the bride was. Even Blake had to agree that Maddie was drop-dead gorgeous. But such beauty was often only surface-deep, he'd found, the same way Lachlan's was.

The same way Claudia's was…

The thought didn't hurt him the way it once had. But that didn't mean he'd forgotten the lessons his one and only marriage had taught him.

The main one was, *Don't, for pity's sake, be-*

lieve anything that ambitious young actresses do or say to you. Sleep with them, by all means, but don't fall for their flattery or their brilliant fakery. And never marry one. Lord, no.

In truth, marriage was not for him—even with a non-ambitious non-actress. Not yet, anyway. Aside from his scepticism over the lasting power of romantic love, he wasn't good husband material. He was way too obsessed with making movies, working seven days a week, often twenty hours a day. What time did that leave for a wife, let alone children?

Maybe when he was forty he might consider both. But he was only just thirty-two. Plenty of years left to think about such things.

Meanwhile, his attention returned to the attractive but bleak-looking bridesmaid.

Damn. She looked as if she was going to cry now. Her bottom lip was definitely quivering, accompanied by a flash of true panic in her eyes. Clearly she didn't *want* to cry. Just in time she got control of herself, her nostrils flaring as she sucked in another deep, desperate breath.

Blake wondered what on earth was going on in that girl's mind. He knew that women often cried at weddings, but they were usually tears of happiness. He could be wrong, he supposed, but he was absolutely certain that whatever she was thinking they weren't happy thoughts!

Maybe this Kate knew what sort of man her kid sister was marrying—knew that he was a player. Maybe she feared for Maddie's future happiness. Well, she had a right to be scared on *that* particular score! Not that he could be a hundred percent positive that was the reason behind her grim face. He could only guess.

In actual fact Blake often found himself speculating on the various emotions he noted on the faces of perfect strangers. He was a people-watcher—an essential talent for a writer-cum-movie-maker. After all, motivations and emotional conflicts were the backbone of all storytelling.

His gaze returned to Kate's stiffly held face and robotic walk. At last she reached the end of the aisle, flashing him a frowning glance before moving sideways to her left, where no one could see her face except the celebrant. And *he* was busy ogling the bride. Now all Blake could see was her profile. Her head and shoulders drooped for a split second, then lifted abruptly, the muscles in her throat standing out as she once again took rigid control of herself.

His heart went out to her. As did his admiration. Whatever was bothering the bride's sister, she was a brave soul. Brave, but still rather fragile.

When the posy of flowers she was holding began to shake Blake determined not to let the evening end before he found out what was upsetting her so much. He could be charming when he wanted to be. And quite good at getting people to open up. Yes, he would worm the truth out of her. Women did love to confide. And hopefully, sooner rather than later, he would bring a smile to her face.

He imagined she would be quite lovely if she smiled. Already Blake found her attractive. And intriguing. And extremely desirable.

Much more desirable than the Barbie doll bride.

CHAPTER TWO

KATE GRITTED HER TEETH, still stunned at how much she was hating this, how sick she felt to her stomach. Yet she'd known for ages that this day was coming. She'd had plenty of time to prepare herself mentally. All to no avail, it seemed.

She clasped her bouquet even tighter and willed her mind to go blank. But her mind refused to obey. It whirled on and on, tormenting her. *Torturing* her.

Because today was the end of the line, wasn't it?

The end of all her hopes and dreams where Lachlan was concerned. Today the man she loved would marry her sister. And that would be that. No more stupidly hoping that he might wake up one morning and realise Maddie wasn't right for him and that *she* was a much more suitable wife. No more fantasising—as she had during their three years studying together at NIDA—that he might finally see her as a potential girlfriend and not just as his good mate and acting buddy.

There was nothing worse, she realised, than the death of hope.

Kate sighed, stiffening when she realised just how loud that sigh had been. As much as she was wretched to her core, she'd determined earlier today not to let anyone—particularly Maddie—suspect the truth. And she'd managed—'til the moment that sickening music had started up and she'd had to step into the spotlight on those stairs. At which point she'd frozen, the sheer futility of her feelings washing through her.

She knew she should have smiled but she simply hadn't been able to. Not that it had mattered. No one had been looking at her. No one except the man standing next to Lachlan. Blake Randall, the best man.

He had kept on looking at her. And frowning at her. Wondering, probably, why she looked so forlorn.

Kate would have liked to tell him why—would have liked to scream that if it hadn't been for *him* all their lives would have taken a different course and she wouldn't be standing here today, having her heart broken.

A slight exaggeration, Kate. Your heart was broken last Christmas, when you optimistically brought Lachlan home for dinner.

They'd both just graduated from NIDA, and Lachlan's parents had gone away on a Christmas cruise. Plus he'd been between girlfriends at the time. Which hadn't happened too often. She'd thought it was her chance to snare his sexual interest. And it had seemed at first that she had. Lachlan had actually flirted with her in the car during their drive from his flat at Bondi to her parents' home at Strathfield.

But all that had changed the moment he'd met her very beautiful and very vivacious blonde sister.

Something had died in Kate when she'd seen how quickly and easily Maddie had captured Lachlan's sexual interest. By the end of Christmas dinner Maddie's almost-fiancé had been firmly dispensed with and she'd gone off with Lachlan, moving in with him the very next day.

So, in reality, Kate had had ten months to get over her broken heart. Ten long, soul-destroying months during which her own acting career had stalled and she'd been reduced to working weekends in a local deli whilst going to endless auditions during the week.

If she hadn't been living at home she wouldn't have survived. The only acting job she'd managed to snare in that time had been a part in a play. It had been quite a good part, too. But the play hadn't proved commercial or popular at the box office. Despite garnering reasonable reviews, it had closed after six weeks.

She'd tried out for various movies and television shows, but had so far been unsuccessful, usually being told that she wasn't 'quite right' for that particular part; didn't have the 'right look'—or the right height, or the right something. Sometimes she wasn't given a reason at all. Her agent said she needed to be more positive when meeting producers and directors, but any positivity she'd possessed seemed to have disintegrated.

In truth, Kate had always been on the shy side, with social skills not her strong point. The only time she felt truly confident was when she was in character, playing an outgoing role. Then she *exuded* confidence. If only she could be more like

Maddie, whose social skills were second to none and whose confidence was out of this world.

A nudge at her elbow snapped her out of her thoughts, and Kate turned to see Maddie glaring at her before shoving her bouquet into her hands. The glare disappeared once she'd turned back to beam at the male celebrant. Kate felt a sudden urge to throw the bridal bouquet onto the floor and stamp on it.

She didn't, of course. But the unexpected burst of anger did achieve something, shoving aside her self-pity and replacing it with a determination to stop letting unrequited love ruin her life. It was way past time for her to get over Lachlan and move on.

Steeling herself, Kate turned her body to the right in order to watch the ceremony, seeing immediately that Blake Randall had done the same and was looking straight at her. No, he was *staring* at her, as if he was trying to work out what was going on in her head.

If she told him he would probably laugh. Whilst she'd never actually met the man, she'd seen him interviewed on television several times. Despite having made a career—and loads of money—

making movies about love and romance, he'd come across as a cynic about both, stating bluntly on one occasion that he was just giving the audience what they wanted.

Of course he had been a popular topic of conversation amongst the students at NIDA—especially after making Lachlan into a star. Kate knew Blake Randall had been married once to Claudia Jay, an Australian actress who'd starred in one of his early films. The marriage hadn't lasted long, and Claudia had claimed her new husband had neglected her shamefully once the honeymoon was over. Kate suspected there was more to their divorce than met the eye, Claudia having moved to Hollywood soon after the breakup.

She didn't feel sorry for either of them. They were both tarred with the same brush, in her opinion. Both of them ruthlessly ambitious, leaving little room to really love anyone other than themselves. Blake had gone from strength to strength after his divorce, whilst Claudia had gone on to have a successful career in Hollywood, her name linked with a succession of high-flying producers and directors.

Kate herself didn't dream of Hollywood success. Or necessarily of being in movies. She loved acting on the stage most of all. But she wouldn't knock back a decent role in a movie or a television series. *If* she was ever offered one.

Kate was about to sigh again when she remembered her agent's advice to be more positive. And a little more proactive. It occurred to her that any other aspiring actor would take advantage of being in a wedding party opposite a brilliant movie-maker like Blake Randall. She shouldn't be ignoring his interested glances. She certainly shouldn't be standing around looking like a wet weekend and sighing all the time. She should be making the most of this rather amazing opportunity by smiling and flirting and projecting Little Miss Confident and Available, not Little Miss Miserable and Vulnerable.

All she had to do was pretend. No, *act*. She *was* an actor, wasn't she?

But it was no use. She simply couldn't summon up a smile. Maybe if he'd been more pleasant and approachable-looking she might have managed it. But his looks matched his reputation as a demanding tyrant to work for. He had gleaming black hair—worn unfashionably long. Thick black brows. Deeply set piercing blue eyes. An arrogant aquiline nose. Slightly hollow cheeks. And a rather cruel-looking mouth.

The press described him as 'handsome'. Kate thought him scary-looking. And very intimidating.

She was in the process of abandoning any idea of even *talking* to him later when he smiled at her. Just a small smile, really—a slight lifting of the corners of his mouth—but it was accompanied by a wicked twinkle in his eyes. They did strange things to her, that smile and that twinkle. Made her feel more confident. And quite sexy. Which was astonishing given her libido seemed to have died ten months ago, along with her heart.

Before she could think better of it she smiled back. A small smile and possibly without any accompanying twinkle. But it was a start. His smile widened, his eyebrows lifting, taking away his scariness and making him look quite handsome. Not handsome the way Lachlan was handsome—but then, no man Kate had ever met was *that* handsome.

He mouthed something at her and she frowned,

not sure what he was saying. He repeated it more slowly and she finally understood the words.

You...look...lovely.

Kate honestly didn't know how to react, blinking her surprise before looking away. She wasn't used to men of Blake Randall's ilk coming on to her. They went for the Maddies of this world. Or for stunning actresses like Claudia Jay. Admittedly she looked the very best she could today—thanks to Maddie and her mother bullying her into hours of work at the beauty salon—but she doubted she could compete with the sort of women who usually vied for this man's attention.

Kate was still trying to work out how to respond when there was a burst of applause behind her. Kate was taken aback to realise that the ceremony was over, and Lachlan and her sister were now legally man and wife.

She waited for a jab of devastation to overwhelm her but it didn't come. Instead all she could think about was Blake Randall flirting with her.

How odd.

There was Maddie in Lachlan's arms, being kissed very thoroughly, and even whilst she couldn't bear to watch at the same time it made her wonder what it would be like to be kissed by that hard, cruel mouth which was once again smiling at her. No, *grinning* at her.

It was infectious, that grin, as was the wry gleam in his eyes as he nodded his head towards the couple who were still locked together in an exhibitionist kiss.

Without thinking this time, she grinned back, and suddenly lightness lifted her previously heavy soul, making her see that there was definitely life after Lachlan.

How silly she'd been to imagine that the world had stopped turning simply because the man she loved did not love her back. There was still plenty to live for. Her career, for starters. Kate adored acting—loved inhabiting another character's skin and making her audience believe that she really was that person. It was the ultimate high when she pulled that off. The ultimate adrenaline rush.

The besotted couple finally wrenched themselves apart, and a flushed Maddie turned to Kate to retrieve her bouquet.

'What a pity Lachlan and I can't leave right now,' her sister grumbled. 'I can hardly wait I'm so turned on. Oh, God, don't look at me like that,

Katie,' she hissed impatiently. 'You know how much I like sex. And my Lachlan is just the *best* at it.'

Kate smothered a groan of despair. Or was it disgust? Whatever it was, that feeling of devastation she'd so valiantly pushed aside was back with a vengeance.

CHAPTER THREE

OH-OH.

Disappointment swamped Blake as he caught sight of Kate again, her face having been obscured by the bride turning to collect her bouquet. Gone was her lovely smile, and in its place her former bleak expression.

What the hell had happened in the last few seconds? What had the Barbie doll said to her? Something not very nice, judging by the unhappiness in Kate's eyes.

Blake knew from first-hand experience that siblings were not always the best of friends—especially those of the same sex. Rivalry and jealousy often raised their ugly heads, making true friendship impossible. His own brother was a case in point. James had always been jealous of him, despite there being absolutely no need. James was the firstborn son, after all, and his parents' favourite—especially since he'd followed in his mother and father's footsteps to become a doctor, like them.

On the other hand Blake had been regarded as the black sheep of the family since he hadn't even gone to university, since he'd done something considered very left field by embracing the entertainment world—first as a DJ, then shooting music videos for a couple of years before finally plunging full-time into making low-budget independent movies.

Both his parents and his brother had given him dire warnings about his future. And Blake found it telling that now he'd made it big they were all hurtfully silent on the subject of his success. Blake had used to let it bother him, but he no longer cared. Or so he told himself. They all had small minds, in his opinion, James the smallest of them all.

Blake rarely saw his family these days, only visiting at Christmas and on special occasions. Now that he'd moved to Los Angeles to live and work he suspected he might not even do that. Just send the occasional card. He no longer kept in contact through social media or email, nor with phone calls, having resolved not to give them any further opportunity to deliver snide remarks about his lifestyle or his movies. Which they did, if given the opportunity.

Blake had no evidence that Kate's sister had just made some kind of nasty remark to her except for the look on her face. But that wasn't jealousy he was seeing in her expressive blue eyes. It was hurt. And dismay.

Why her unhappiness bothered him so much he could not fathom. He'd never been a particularly empathetic soul. Perhaps it was because he found her attractive and didn't like the idea of there being some hidden impediment which would hinder his pursuing his interest in her. Whatever the reason, Blake resolved not to rest until he'd solved the mystery of that unhappiness.

And it *was* a mystery. Because on the surface of things Kate had nothing to be unhappy about. She was gorgeous! Okay, she didn't have the in-your-face blonde beauty of her sister. But she was still highly desirable.

Of course being physically attractive was no guarantee of happiness. Maybe she was unhappy because she was still unmarried, despite being the older sister. Though not much older, surely. Blake knew Lachlan's bride was only twenty-three, which made Kate what? Twenty-five? Twenty-six, maybe? Hardly a marital use-by date in this day and age.

'Get with the programme, Blake,' Lachlan said, grabbing his nearest elbow. 'We have to sign the marriage certificate.'

As the groom ushered him over to where the paperwork had been set up on a side table Blake cast a surreptitious glance back at Kate. She seemed to have gathered herself, and her expression was not wretched any longer. It was, however, utterly devoid of emotion once more—a totally blank mask. How on earth did she manage that? When *he* was upset everyone knew about it. He didn't throw tantrums, exactly, but his face always reflected his feelings—as did his voice.

He watched her watching the happy couple sign the register, but her eyes betrayed nothing now. Which was telling in itself.

When it was their turn to step forward as witnesses, he waved for her to go first. After throwing him a closed look, she picked up one of the provided pens and signed quickly, with only the slightest tremor in her hand. He glanced at her signature before he signed his own name.

Kate Holiday, he read, and realised that until that moment he hadn't known the bride's surname. So of course he hadn't known Kate's. He'd never met the bride's parents either, or anyone else in her family. Strange, really, given he was the best man.

Blake wondered all of a sudden why Lachlan had asked *him* to be his best man. He would have thought a young Aussie male with his looks and personality would have had at least one best mate—a pal he'd gone to school with or studied at NIDA with.

Obviously not. Either that or he preferred someone famous to stand by his side at his wedding. A celebrity. Lachlan was very much into celebrity.

It hadn't occurred to Blake until that moment that he was being used—that this wedding was little more than a publicity stunt, with a trophy bride, a glamorous Sydney setting and a rich and famous best man. Lachlan was no better than Claudia, really.

Whilst the thought did bring a sour note to the proceedings Blake knew he would have the last laugh. Because in actual fact Lachlan wasn't so great an actor, and his range was decidedly limited. Once he was seduced by the big boys in Hollywood and started making movies that weren't tailored to his specific brand of looks and charm his career might very well sink like a stone. Major studios were very unforgiving once the box office results rolled in. Lachlan's past successes in Blake's movies would not carry him for ever.

A slight smirk curved his top lip as he put his signature to the marriage certificate. It was still there when he put the pen down and turned to face his intriguing partner.

'So, Kate Holiday,' he said, doing his best to hide his underlying irritation, 'we haven't been properly introduced. But I dare say you know who I am.'

'Yes, of course I do,' Kate said. 'Lachlan has spoken of you a lot.'

'Well, you have one up on me, then—because he's told me nothing about you.'

She seemed quite taken aback. 'You mean he's never mentioned that we were students together at NIDA? We were in the same class,' she went on, obviously peeved. 'We graduated together last year.'

'Sorry. He's never mentioned it,' he told her, doing his best to get his head around this news.

Kate was an *actress*! Who would have believed it? Still, it went some way to explaining her ability to hide her emotions. Though she wasn't hiding them at the moment. She was looking decidedly upset. On his part, he was just perplexed.

Why hadn't Lachlan told him that his future sister-in-law had been at NIDA with him? He knew Blake held an enormous respect for their graduates. On top of that, he was always on the lookout for fresh talent—especially actors with Kate's unique and very interesting face.

He wondered if Lachlan was jealous of her acting talent. That would be just like him. He would hate anyone to steal his thunder. Narcissistic devil!

'All I know is that you're Maddie's older sister,' he admitted. 'I don't even know how much older.'

'I'm twenty-five,' she confessed, almost as if it was a crime.

Twenty-five was a good age for an actress, he thought. And for other things...

Finding out that Kate was an actress didn't

dampen his desire for her in any way. If anything, it increased it—along with his sudden resolve to help her career in any way he could. Blake suspected it might not have taken off, since he'd never heard of Kate Holiday. And he would have if she'd done anything of note. Blake had his finger on the pulse where rising stars were concerned.

Just then they were shepherded outside by the photographer—a rather officious fellow who was very full of himself.

'So, what have you been in lately?' he asked her as they trailed past the huge marquee which had been set up in the gorgeous grounds of Byron's home. 'Anything I might have seen?'

'I doubt it,' she said. 'I was in a play earlier this year, but it closed rather quickly. I was brilliant, of course,' Kate added, throwing a self-deprecating smile his way. 'But not brilliant enough, apparently. One of the reviews said I was "very decorative".'

Blake laughed. 'Which you are,' he said. 'Very.'

She looked startled, her high cheekbones pinkening a little. Acting? he wondered. Or was she genuinely taken aback by his compliment? Blake decided he didn't care either way. She enchanted him. And intrigued him. He was going to enjoy finding out more about her this evening, and at the same time putting a spoke in Lachlan's ego by giving her career a boost.

He would offer her a part in one of his upcoming movies. Nothing too large. She was an unknown, after all.

Of course Blake anticipated that his offer to help her out would come with the bonus of taking her to bed in the foreseeable future. Which he very much wanted to do. More so than he had in a long while. Whilst sex was something he enjoyed, he wasn't a sex addict. He could do without—especially when he was working long hours. Which he had been for several weeks now, finishing up Lachlan's latest movie and getting it ready for distribution.

Possibly this longish stint of celibacy was responsible for the rather urgent wave of desire he was currently experiencing. Hopefully there wasn't any extraneous reason why Kate shouldn't respond to his pursuit. The only hurdle he could think of was a boyfriend in the wings. Or, worse, a fiancé.

A swift glance at her left hand detected a total absence of rings.

Good. A boyfriend he could handle, but a fiancé was another matter entirely.

'I am *so* going to hate these photographs,' Kate muttered when the photographer started giving them orders.

'I don't know why,' he commented as they were forcefully arranged in a group in the well-lit gazebo, with the harbour and the bridge in the background. 'With your bone structure I bet you're very photogenic.'

Even if she wasn't the best actress in the world, she would look good on screen. Blake felt confident that the camera would love her.

'It's very nice of you to say so.'

'Not at all. It's the truth. I never say things just to be nice.'

Not until tonight, that is. For some weird and wonderful reason Blake felt uncharacteristically compelled to be nice to Kate. *Very* nice. And it wasn't just because he wanted to have sex with her. Right from the first moment he'd set eyes on her sad-looking self she'd brought out the gallant in him. Which was unusual. Because a white knight with women Blake was *not*—especially since Claudia's betrayal.

Quite frankly he could be a bit of a bastard where the opposite sex was concerned. Especially if the girl was an ambitious young actress who made it obvious when they met that she was his for the taking—not because of a genuine attraction but because sleeping with him would further her career.

Kate was different, though. A different sort of girl. A different sort of actress.

He'd given her every opportunity to flirt with him. And flatter him. But she'd done neither. He liked that. He liked that a lot.

'Would the bridesmaid please *smile*?' the photographer snapped impatiently. 'This is a wedding, not a funeral.'

CHAPTER FOUR

BUT IT IS a funeral, Kate wanted to wail. It was the death of her dream to marry Lachlan herself one day.

A stupid dream, really. Stupid and futile—especially once he'd met Maddie.

Of course she should never have taken him home. But she'd honestly thought it would be safe, with Maddie practically engaged. How had she been supposed to know that they would take one look at each other and fall head over heels in love?

Well, you should have known, you idiot!

Not that it would have made any difference.

Get real, you fool. Even before he met Maddie Lachlan had three years to notice you in that way. But he didn't and he never would have! You're not his type—which is blonde and beautiful, with buckets of self-esteem and a sense of self-entitlement to rival royalty. Somehow that description doesn't fit you, dear heart. Not even remotely.

A very strong male arm suddenly wound around her waist, pulling her firmly against his side and propelling Kate out of her self-pitying thoughts. Glancing up at Blake, she encountered narrowed blue eyes giving her a warning look.

'If you don't start smiling properly,' he whispered into her ear, 'I'll start thinking you can't act your way out of a paper bag.'

Kate blinked, then swallowed and straightened her spine—after which she rewarded him with a beaming smile. Because no way did she want Blake Randall thinking she couldn't act. Hadn't she resolved earlier to try to use the opportunity of meeting him to her advantage? It would be utterly foolish to ignore a man of his influence and contacts. If she couldn't have Lachlan's love, then at least she could have a career.

'That's better,' he said, smiling down at her.

Her spirits lifted again, as they had earlier when he'd smiled at her. Kate couldn't quite understand why he was as interested in her as he seemed to be—but who was she to look a gift horse in the mouth?

The photos were still a trial—especially when she and Blake mostly had to stand to one side and witness Maddie and Lachlan having endless shots taken of just the two of them in all sorts of romantic poses and clinches.

Maddie had confessed to Kate that morning that they'd already sold their wedding photos to a well-known tabloid—which wasn't surprising. Her sister was very money-hungry. Celebrity-hungry, too. They were certainly a well-matched couple in that regard; Kate was well aware of Lachlan's love of fame.

She winced as she watched him kiss his blushing bride for the umpteenth time.

If she'd been alone with Blake, Kate might have been able to distract herself by chatting about movies. But, no, fate wasn't going to be that kind. Her parents were now hurrying over to them, demanding to be introduced, and gushing like mad over the bride and groom.

After what felt like for ever, but was probably only a few minutes, Blake suddenly took her arm and said, 'You must excuse us, folks, but we really have to speak to Byron ASAP.'

He didn't explain further, just swept a relieved Kate away.

'Are they always like that?' he growled as he snatched two glasses of champagne from a passing waiter, pressing one into Kate's hand.

'Like what?'

'Raving about your sister like she's a bloody princess. They never said a word about how gorgeous *you* look. It was all about Maddie—Little Miss Perfect and oh, so clever to have snared herself a husband like Lachlan.' He snorted at that. 'They won't be saying that in a couple of years' time.'

'What do you mean?' she asked, a little flustered by his saying *she* looked gorgeous.

'Damn it,' he said, gulping his glass of champagne before giving her a slightly sheepish look. 'I probably shouldn't be saying this. Though maybe you already suspect?'

'Suspect what?'

'That where the opposite sex is concerned Lachlan is a rat. No, more of a cat. A tom cat. He can't keep it in his pants for long. Trust me when I say that being married won't stop him from sleeping around. I walked in on him having sex with a make-up girl just a few weeks ago. Long after his engagement to your sister.'

Possibly Kate shouldn't have been shocked—Lachlan had garnered quite a reputation during his years at NIDA—but she was.

'Poor Maddie,' she said, and downed half of her glass of champagne.

'I agree with you. If she truly loves Lachlan then she's in for a bumpy road.'

What an odd thing to say, Kate thought. *If she truly loves him.* Of course Maddie truly loved him. Lachlan was the sort of man who inspired love. Every time Kate looked at him she felt that tightening in her stomach, that wave of longing. So nowadays she tried not to look at him. It was easier that way.

She did go and see his movies, though. Which was the worst form of masochism since they were all love stories and always had at least one sex scene. But she simply could not resist.

'Is that why you were upset earlier?' Byron asked her. 'Because you're worried about your sister's future happiness?'

Kate stared up into his deeply set blue eyes, which held a surprisingly sympathetic expression at that moment. And there she'd been, believing he was some kind of ruthless bastard. Not so, it seemed.

'Yes,' she lied, for how could she tell him that it was her own future happiness that had been worrying her?

He reached out to touch her wrist lightly. 'No point in worrying about other people's marriages. What will be will be.'

Kate didn't know what to think. Her thoughts were somewhat scattered. How could Lachlan do something like that? It had certainly tarnished her opinion of him. Not her love, however. That didn't tarnish quite so easily.

Suddenly she frowned at Blake. 'Why did you agree to be Lachlan's best man when it's obvious you don't like him very much?'

He shrugged. 'Don't get me wrong. I don't dislike Lachlan. He's not a bad fellow. Just weak when it comes to women throwing themselves at him. Which they do. All the time. Look, he asked me to be his best man and I said yes. Call it a business move rather than a measure of close friendship. The publicity will be good for our next movie, which should be coming out in the New

Year. Too late, unfortunately, to be up for any awards this year, but I couldn't get it edited and distributed any earlier.'

'I see. And is that also why you organised for the wedding to be held here? For the added publicity?'

'No. I didn't think of that at the time. When the other venue burnt down we still had a couple of weeks' shooting to complete in Hawaii, and I couldn't afford for my leading man to keep getting hysterical phone calls from his fiancée. So I stepped in and fixed things. Now, I think they're waiting for us to go into the marquee for the reception. We'll be on the same table, but I doubt we're seated side by side—worst luck. Still, there'll be a party and dancing afterwards. Then we can talk some more.'

He put a firm hand in the small of her back and gently pushed her towards the entrance to the marquee. It felt good, that hand. Very...*reassuring*. Also very intimate.

She sneaked a quick glance up into his deep blue eyes, startled when they bored back down into hers with the sort of lustful look men usually reserved for Maddie.

The realisation that Blake Randall lusted after *her* was flattering, but also very flustering. Her whole body tightened in response, which threw her. She couldn't *possibly* lust after Blake Randall in return, could she? Surely not. She was just shocked, that was all.

And yet…

She glanced over at him again, this time focusing on his mouth and recalling how she'd wondered earlier in the proceedings what it would be like to kiss him.

Exciting, she decided, her heartbeat quickening. Exciting and risky. *Very* risky. Because he wouldn't want to stop at kissing.

Kate knew in theory that love and lust didn't have to reside together. But she'd never experienced one without the other. Which was why her very limited forays into sex had been such disasters—and why, for the last four years, she hadn't had a proper boyfriend or been to bed with anyone. How could she after falling so deeply in love with Lachlan?

Yet as she stared at Blake Randall's perversely sexy mouth she could not dismiss the notion that she just might enjoy going to bed with him despite not loving him. Not that she would. She wasn't that sort of girl. She wasn't like Maddie, who'd been jumping into men's beds at the drop of a hat since she was sixteen.

Besides, you don't really want to go to bed with him, Kate told herself firmly. *You're just flattered that he fancies you. That's what this is all about. Not true lust. Just your poor pathetic ego, desperate for someone to show some interest in you. Now, stop ogling the man and get some perspective!*

Just in time she wrenched her eyes away from his mouth. But it was too late. His lips were drawing back into a knowing smile. He'd already seen her staring at him.

'First dance is mine,' he said with a devilish twinkle in his eyes. 'Don't forget.'

Relief claimed Kate as the wedding planner bustled over to them, interrupting what was becoming an awkward situation.

Her name was Clare. She was about fifty, a sleekly attractive blonde with an air of self-importance somewhat like the photographer's. They were in business together, Maddie's mother having hired them because they were supposedly 'the best'.

'*Do* come along, Kate,' the woman said, and glanced at her watch. 'You too, Mr Randall. We are now running behind schedule.'

Blake rolled his eyes at Kate after Clare had departed to hurry up some of the other guests.

'Irritating woman,' he muttered as he steered Kate over to their table. 'Do you know she had the hide to ask to see my speech? Claimed she needed to check if it was too long.'

'How rude!'

'That's what I thought. Lord knows how people like that stay in business. Anyway, I didn't show it to her because I haven't written one. I just assured her it would be the shortest best man's speech in history. Which it will be. I detest long speeches.'

Kate gnawed at her bottom lip. 'You're not going to say anything...revealing, are you?'

'About Lachlan being a player, you mean?'

'Yes.'

'Of course not. That's not my place. My role tonight is to be complimentary and charming and funny.' Blake laughed at the doubtful look on her face. 'Don't worry. I can be all of those things when I need to be. I'm actually a very good actor myself.'

CHAPTER FIVE

BLAKE WAS AS good as his word, keeping his best man's speech very short and very witty, heaping gushing compliments on the bride and hearty praise on the groom, refraining from any of the usual tasteless *double entendres* concerning the groom's past behaviour with the opposite sex, and finishing up by toasting the happy couple with gusto.

I really am a good actor, he decided when he sat down to huge applause less than five minutes after he'd stood up. Because it had certainly gone against the grain for him to say the overly nice things he had. He hadn't lied for Lachlan's sake, of course, or for the bride, but for Kate, whom he could see had been upset by his revelation about Lachlan's lack of morals.

He regretted telling her now. It had been unnecessary. He'd achieved nothing except to increase her anxiety over the future of her sister's happiness. Clearly she was fond of her sister, despite her parents' obvious favouritism for the younger girl.

He cringed when he recalled the father of the bride's over-effusive speech about his perfect younger daughter. It had been sick-making. If he'd been Kate he would have walked out. Or thrown something at him. But she'd just sat there, sipping champagne and smiling, even laughing at some of her father's gushing stories about Maddie as a little girl.

She was an incredibly generous and sweet-natured soul. Odd, given her chosen career. Aspiring actresses were rarely sweet. Unless they were faking it. And Blake felt confident she wasn't.

He smiled when he thought of her smallish breasts and her lack of false eyelashes. No. Nothing fake about Kate Holiday.

Which was one of the reasons he found her so attractive.

She found him attractive too.

Blake was an expert in female body language, and he'd noticed her reaction to his none-too-subtle compliments. She liked them, but didn't quite know how to react to them. Didn't seem to know how to flirt.

Not like her sister. He might not have met the bride before, but he'd seen her in action tonight— both with the celebrant and the photographer and also himself, to a degree. Not that she'd actually said anything to him yet. There'd been no opportunity. But she'd fluttered her false eyelashes at him whenever she'd had a chance, her smile both sweetly coy and smoulderingly sexy at the same time.

She was a piece of work, all right. Lachlan just might have met his match with Maddie Holiday.

Finally the interminable meal and the speeches were over and the happy couple rose, leaving the table to go and cut their three-tiered wedding cake.

Blake immediately moved into the bride's vacant chair so that he could talk to Kate. 'So what did you think?' he asked her on a teasing note. 'Did my speech meet with your approval?'

She smiled at him, her expression wry. 'You're right. You're a *very* good actor. You didn't mean a single word of it, did you?'

'I meant the bit I slipped in about the beautiful bridesmaid. I didn't think the groom complimented you enough in his speech. Now, the dancing will start soon. I've been to a few weddings in my time, so I know the routine. First the bride and groom will do the bridal waltz, and then we'll all be invited to join them on the dance floor.'

'Yes, I know,' she said. 'I have been to the odd wedding or two as well. Though never as a bridesmaid.'

'Never?' That surprised him, given her age and her niceness. 'But you must have loads of girlfriends. Haven't any of them got married yet?'

'Actually, no,' she said.

'No, you haven't got loads of girlfriends? Or no, none of them have got married yet?'

'I do have a few girlfriends from my years at NIDA, but no one so close that they would ask me to be a bridesmaid.'

'What about from school?'

'No. I wasn't popular at school. I was considered a nerd. And not very cool.'

'I find that hard to believe,' he said, but he was lying.

He could see that she was on the reserved, rather introverted side. *He'd* been very popular at school—perhaps because he'd been a rebel. There was no rebel in Kate. Not a great deal of confidence, either. How on earth did she expect to succeed as an actress if she didn't exude confidence?

Still, she had *him* to help her now. She just didn't know it yet. It was probably not the right time or place to offer her a part in one of his movies tonight. Or to try to seduce her, either.

But he couldn't let the grass grow under his feet. He was flying back to LA in a few days. And Blake had no intention of going back without having some delicious sex with this delightful creature, as well as giving her career a much-needed boost.

He would invite her out to dinner tomorrow night. Somewhere seriously good. After which he would take her back to the city penthouse he was staying in. It belonged to Byron, but he wasn't using it much now that he'd moved into this absolutely gorgeous harbour-side mansion.

'What about boyfriends?' he asked, wanting to know the lie of the land before he got his hopes up too high. Not that a boyfriend would stop him now. The more time he spent with Kate the more he wanted her.

'What?' she said, blinking up at him.

God, she did have lovely eyes. And so expressive. Perfect for the camera.

'You said you don't have loads of girlfriends,' he went on, 'but you've surely had loads of boyfriends. There must be one at the moment.'

A strange cloud dulled her eyes. Strange, because he couldn't read the emotion behind it. What *was* it? Not distress. Or dismay. Sadness again? Yes, that was it. Sadness. A very deep sadness. He wondered if she'd had a serious boyfriend and something dreadful had happened to him. He couldn't imagine any man worth his salt dumping Kate, so what else could it be?

Only death, Blake decided, warranted this depth of sadness. A very recent death, possibly. That would explain everything that had puzzled him about her tonight. It might also explain why she hadn't responded all that strongly to his none-too-subtle overtures. Perhaps by finding him attractive—and he was pretty sure she did—she felt she was betraying her loved one.

Blake pulled himself up sharply before he got carried away. Which he did sometimes. Nothing worse than being a movie-maker. He found drama in every situation. The reality was probably nothing like what he was imagining.

'Actually, no,' she said, a rueful little smile hovering. 'I do not have a boyfriend at the moment. I have had boyfriends in the past, of course.'

Well of course she had. If she hadn't she wouldn't be normal.

'Then there's no one to object if I ask you out to dinner tomorrow night?' he went on.

She didn't look totally surprised, just a little wary.

'No,' she said, but there was reservation in her voice and reluctance in her eyes.

He knew then that she wasn't going to be easily seduced. One part of him admired her for it, but that other part—the part which was aching and hard and more conscienceless than it had ever been—refused to be deterred.

So he decided to play his trump card. Too bad if it was a bit premature. A man had to do what a man had to do.

'I want to talk to you about a part in my next movie which I think would be perfect for you,' he added, dangling what he knew would be a powerful carrot.

There was no doubting her surprise. No, her *shock*. Genuine, ingenuous shock. God, she really was irresistible.

'But why would you do that?' she asked, jerking her head back a little as she blinked up at him. 'Surely you would need me to audition for you first.'

Damn it all, why did she have to be so difficult? He respected her for it, but it was irritating.

'I don't need to see an audition from a graduate of NIDA,' he dismissed. 'Their programme produces the most talented actors.'

'Yes, but…but…'

'Kate Holiday,' he said sternly. 'Do you want to be a successful actress or not?'

'Of course I do,' she replied, looking quite offended. 'It's what I want most in the world.'

'Then stop looking a gift horse in the mouth.'

She smiled then. Which pleased him no end.

'You'll come to dinner tomorrow night?'

'Yes.'

'Good. Now, let's go and dance.'

CHAPTER SIX

HOW AMAZING, KATE thought a little breathlessly as Blake swept her onto the dance floor and into his arms. Dinner tomorrow night and a part in a Blake Randall movie.

Amazing, but also a little worrying. She'd heard casting couch stories, knew that it still happened, and wondered if Blake was of that ilk. Would he expect her to have sex with him at the end of the evening?

Kate knew he fancied her—had seen desire in his eyes. And even more worrying was the suspicion that if he made a pass at her she might just say yes to whatever he wanted. Which was not like her at all!

But this was her chance, wasn't it? she reasoned desperately. Her chance to get her career off the ground. And she did find him attractive. Very attractive. And sexy. *Very* sexy. It was that mouth of his. And the hot, hungry gleam which fired up his eyes whenever he looked down at her. Which he was doing at the moment. He made her feel sexy in return. And terribly tempted.

A thought suddenly came to her, however—one she didn't like at all.

'This part you have in mind for me,' she said as he whirled her round, thankfully at arm's length. 'It's not in one of Lachlan's movies, is it? I honestly don't want to be in one of his movies.'

'No, it's not a rom-com. More of a family drama. A character-based script which I wrote a few years ago but hadn't got round to making. But it's all systems go now, and we start shooting in late November. Look, keep this under your hat, but I think Lachlan and I will be parting company in the near future.'

'But why?' she asked, totally taken aback.

Blake glanced over at the man in question before answering. Fortunately the dance floor was big enough for them not to be too close. Nevertheless, when he spoke he kept his voice low.

'Mr Rodgers has an exalted opinion of his acting abilities. He doesn't really understand why his movies with me have been so successful. He thinks it's solely due to him. He might do one more movie with me, but he'll go with the money in the end. He recently got himself a new agent— one who's buddy-buddy with the big production companies. They've already offered him a very lucrative contract for three movies. He says he's just thinking about it, but I can see the writing on the wall.'

'That's not very loyal of him,' Kate said, feeling upset for Blake. Though he didn't seem that upset himself.

He shrugged. 'There's no such thing as loyalty in Hollywood. Just box office figures. I'll survive without him, I can assure you. I have several new projects already in the pipeline—none of which rely on Lachlan Rodgers.'

'That's good.'

Good, too, that she wouldn't have to work with him. That would have been just awful. And so would her acting have been, with her new brother-in-law's presence being both distracting and up-setting.

Still, Blake might be right about Lachlan's acting abilities being limited. When they'd been at NIDA he certainly hadn't come top of the class. He'd been good, but not as good as some of the others. She herself had been singled out by their teachers for more praise than he had.

'Let's not talk about Lachlan any more,' Blake said. 'I'd rather talk about you. So, tell me, if you've only had that one part in a play since you graduated, how have you been surviving financially?'

'Well, I do live at home, rent-free. And I've been working at a local deli at the weekends. That pays for my clothes and fares, and leaves me free to go to auditions during the week.'

'Do you have a good agent?'

Kate sighed. 'I thought I did. But I'm beginning to have my doubts.'

'You need to get yourself a new one, then.'

'I think I will.'

The music changed from a waltz to a faster, more throbbing beat. More people got up to dance, at which point Blake pulled Kate very close and told her to put her arms around his neck. After a slight hesitation she did so, and felt Blake dropping his hands down to her hips. His grip was firm, pulling her lower half against him, making Kate quickly aware of something hard pressing against her stomach. It was impossible to ignore.

Blake's eyelids grew heavy with the contact, and a tense silence enveloped them as their fused hips swayed to the music. On her part she felt mesmerised—both by the obvious evidence of his desire for her and her own shocking thoughts. She began imagining how it would feel to have his flesh buried deep inside hers, to have his mouth on hers, kissing her, only lifting to whisper hot, hungry words in her ear.

Her mouth went dry.

Not so another part of her anatomy.

Suddenly she needed to go to the bathroom. ASAP.

'I'm sorry,' she said, flustered by the urgency of that need, not to mention what was going on in her head. 'But I... I have to go to the Ladies. Too much champagne.'

A total lie. She'd only had one glass during dinner, worried that if she drank too much she might do something she'd regret, might somehow make a total fool of herself.

It had taken every ounce of her acting ability not to react to her father's speech, not to let jealousy for Maddie take her over. She loved her sister. She always had. But she did so hate it that everyone else loved her so *much*, with no love left over for her. Lachlan's speech had been total agony, and Kate hadn't been able to look at him even when he'd toasted *her*, as was his duty.

'Sorry,' she repeated, and then hurried away out of the marquee, almost running back to the house and up the staircase to the bedroom and en-suite bathroom where she'd dressed earlier.

There was probably a powder room or two downstairs, but she didn't know where they were and she simply couldn't wait. But, perversely, when she sat on the toilet she didn't do all that much, and yet the odd feeling of pressure remained.

She'd never felt anything quite like it. Not painful, exactly. No, not painful at all. Just weirdly tight and tense. Her belly was as hard as a rock, whilst elsewhere she was hot and embarrassingly wet. Once again her thoughts took flight, her fantasies definitely on the R-rated side.

'Good grief, Kate,' she groaned aloud, confused by the way she could want any man like this, when she was in love with someone else.

She certainly hadn't done so for the last four years. Never. Not once. Blake Randall, however, seemed to have broken through her frozen libido and brought it to life in a startling way. More than startling when she considered that even when she'd first fallen in love with Lachlan he hadn't evoked so violent a physical reaction.

Her feelings about him had always seemed more softly romantic than starkly sexual. She sighed over him. And dreamt about him. But she'd never been consumed by explicit sexual fantasies. Which she had been a minute ago.

Kate shuddered as she recalled that moment when she'd literally ached to have sex with Blake. She was still aching.

Oh, Lord, whatever was she going to do?

You're going to get a grip, that's what you're going to do. Then go back downstairs and...

And what?

She honestly had no idea. She'd probably leave it up to Blake to make the next move. And he would. She felt sure of it. And the prospect was sending an excited shiver down her spine.

After she'd washed her hands she stared at herself in the vanity mirror, seeing her over-bright eyes and flushed cheeks. Glancing down, she checked to see if her nipples were on show. Thankfully they weren't, courtesy of the corset-style underwear she had on. Maddie had chosen it for her, insisting that it would give her some shape. Which, right now, she was grateful it did.

Kate couldn't deny that she wanted Blake to pursue her. What she *didn't* want was for her own desire to be embarrassingly obvious, or for him to think any response of hers was because he had offered to give her a part in one of his movies. Because what she was feeling at the moment had nothing to do with her career and everything to do with herself as a woman.

It was quite thrilling to be the centre of attention for a change. To feel special, and attractive, and truly desired.

At the same time Kate still felt flustered by the strength of her own sexual response to Blake's overtures. She didn't quite know what to do next. Flirting didn't come naturally to her. She wasn't like Maddie. She didn't have her sister's sexual boldness. Or her confidence. What if she was misreading the situation?

This last thought brought a laugh to her lips. How could she possibly have misread that erection? Unless, of course—she giggled a little—Blake had a gun in his pocket.

Kate had a smile on her lips as she left the bathroom—a smile which was wiped away when she encountered Lachlan standing in the bedroom, with a dark scowl on his beautifully shaped mouth.

'Lachlan!' she exclaimed. 'What are you doing here? Where's Maddie?'

'Dancing with your father. She won't miss me for a minute or two. I told her I was going to the Gents. Look, I saw you duck out of the marquee and I followed you.'

Kate frowned. 'But why?'

'I wanted a word with you in private. I wanted to warn you.'

'Warn me? About what?'

'About Blake bloody Randall.'

Kate sucked in sharply. Why on earth was Lachlan speaking about his mentor and best man with such disrespect? 'What…what about him?'

'About his modus operandi with pretty women—especially ones who have acting in their blood.'

Kate was torn between being flattered by Lachlan calling her pretty and worrying about what this dreaded 'modus operandi' could be. Though she was beginning to suspect…

'First things first: does he know you went to NIDA with me?'

'Well, yes, he does. I told him.'

'*Damn*. That's stuffed things good and proper, then. No doubt he's already offered you a part in one of his movies? That's one of his moves when he fancies an actress. And you're looking extra-fanciable tonight, Kate. Frankly, I've never seen you looking so good. Blake only goes for the good-looking ones. So, *has* he offered you a part?'

'Well, yes,' she admitted, feeling a little bit sick. 'A small one.'

'I don't doubt it's just a small one,' Lachlan scoffed. 'Mr Perfectionist wouldn't risk spoiling one of his movies by giving an unknown a seriously *good* part. You'll probably only have a few words here and there. Just enough to make sure you have to be on location with him so that he can shag you every night. But once the movie is wrapped up you can bet that will be the end of it. He has a reputation for seducing his female stars, but once the movie is over so is the affair.'

He came forward and curved his hands over her shoulders—a gesture that shocked Kate rigid because it forced her to look up into his eyes…those beautiful blue eyes which had entranced her from the first day they'd met.

Perversely, however, neither his touch nor his proximity sent her weak at the knees, as she might have expected. All she felt was a confused wariness.

'I wouldn't like to see that happen to you, Kate,' he went on. 'You're far too nice a girl to be used by that bastard.'

Goodness. Such strong words! 'Is that why you didn't tell Blake I was in your class at NIDA?' she asked, trying to make sense of Lachlan's present attitude, not to mention his past actions. 'You were trying to protect me?'

That startled him, and his hands dropped away as he stepped back in surprise. It took him a few seconds to school his face into an expression of concern. 'Well, yes. Yes…yes, of *course* that's why,' he said, hurriedly but not convincingly.

Kate wasn't sure what to believe now—both about Blake's so-called bad reputation with actresses and Lachlan's using it as an excuse for not mentioning her to Blake at any stage. Nothing rang true.

Okay, so Blake offering her a part without auditioning her had been surprising. In all honesty, however, she couldn't see Blake having to bribe girls into his bed. He was the sort of man women would throw themselves at. She herself was already wildly attracted to him.

'I find it hard to believe Blake is as bad as you say he is,' Kate said.

Lachlan's bedroom blue eyes softened on her and he once again reached to curve his hands around her shoulders. 'Oh, Kate, Kate… Trust me when I say you don't want to get tangled up with Blake Randall. He can be a twisted bastard. That bitch Claudia throwing him over totally screwed him up. He likes breaking hearts—especially when that heart belongs to an actress. He's bad news, sweetheart. Promise me you won't take him up on his offer—that you'll be having nothing further to do with him after tonight.'

Kate shook her head from side to side, her thoughts more muddled than ever. 'Why did you ask him to be your best man if you despise him so much?' she asked, in an echo of what she'd asked Blake earlier.

Lachlan shrugged. 'It was a good publicity move to promote our next movie. On top of that he was chuffed by my asking. Look, you can't afford to get on the wrong side of the right people in the movie-making world, so don't go telling him I said any of this. Just don't accept that part, for pity's sake. Tell him you don't want to make movies...that you'd rather act on the stage. That's what you always said you wanted to do.'

'I do. But I haven't been very successful at it, in case you haven't noticed.'

'What? Oh, yes. That's bad luck. Still, if you show up at auditions in future looking the way you look tonight you should be in like Flynn. Now, I really must go. Lord, but you *do* look delicious...'

He bent and gave her a peck on the cheek before dashing out of the room and running down the stairs back to his beautiful bride, leaving Kate's head in total turmoil. Because she simply couldn't believe in Lachlan's sudden concern for her. He'd hardly even spoken to her this past year, and had never asked her how things were going for her career-wise.

Not that she'd seen him all that often, but there had been the odd occasion. A family dinner last Easter. A Mother's Day luncheon in May. Then his and Maddie's engagement party a few months ago...

Maybe his dislike of Blake's behaviour with women *was* a credible reason why he hadn't told his mentor about her. But she didn't buy it. She was beginning to suspect that Lachlan didn't want to share his success—that he wanted to be the only one in his class to make it big in the movies.

Kate's love for Lachlan didn't blind her to his faults. Behind his charm lay considerable arrogance, a selfish nature and a rather ruthless ambition. She was glad now that she hadn't made him any rash promises, because in all honesty she didn't *want* to turn down the part. It was a chance to show someone with lots of connections and contacts that she could act.

Okay, so Blake could be a devil with women. That didn't really surprise her, given his success and his power. But forewarned *was* forearmed. And she didn't have to sleep with him if she didn't want to. The trouble was...she *did*, actually. If Kate were strictly honest with herself, the idea of Blake Randall seducing her was not altogether an unattractive prospect. As for him sending her on her way with a broken heart... Well, that part was laughable. Impossible. Her heart had already been broken.

So to hell with being sweet and nice, plus a total failure. It was time to take a few risks. Time to be proactive, the way her agent kept telling her to be. Time to stop being lily-livered and put her best foot forward!

CHAPTER SEVEN

WHERE ON EARTH *was* she? Blake began thinking when Kate didn't return after ten minutes. How long did it take for a girl to go to the toilet?

Lifting his champagne to his lips, he took a deep swallow, thinking all the while that if she didn't show in the next thirty seconds he would go in search of her.

'Not like you to be standing alone at a party,' Byron said as he wandered up to him, looking splendid in his tux.

But then, Byron would look good in anything. The man had everything. Looks. Money. Charm. And more recently a gorgeous wife and a delightful baby girl. Blake would have been jealous of the man if he didn't like him so much. And if he wasn't such a solid investor in his movies.

'I'm waiting for my dancing partner to come back from the powder room,' he grumbled. 'She's been gone ages.'

'I presume you're talking about Kate?'

'Yes, Kate.'

'Sweet girl. Much sweeter than her sister,' Byron observed drily.

'Too true,' Blake agreed. 'I wouldn't want to be married to *that* one.'

Byron laughed. 'You wouldn't want to be married to *anyone.*'

'You know me so well. Ah, here she is. Kate, sweetheart, what took you so long?'

Kate had no intention of telling him the truth. Certainly not in front of Byron. Or ever, actually.

She grabbed a glass of champagne from a passing waiter and smiled at the two men over the rim as she took a long swallow. They were the sort of men that women must smile at a lot, she conceded. Both very attractive, though in entirely different ways. Byron was fair-haired and traditionally handsome, with clean-cut even features and a smile which might out-dazzle Lachlan's. He was a true gentleman. Whereas Blake looked more like a gypsy, with his wayward black hair, his dark beetling eyebrows and deeply set and very intense eyes.

They pierced her now, those eyes, making her

quiver inside. *Lord, but he wouldn't have to try too hard to seduce me,* came the shocking thought.

'Kate's an actress—did you know?' Blake asked Byron, whilst not taking his eyes off her.

Byron's eyebrows lifted. 'No, I didn't know.'

'Neither did I until tonight. She's a graduate of NIDA. Was in the same class as Lachlan.'

'Really? How come he didn't mention it?'

'I have no idea.'

Once again Kate kept silent. After all, what could she say? She really wasn't sure what reason was behind her supposed good friend not mentioning her acting aspirations. But she suspected it had nothing to do with protecting her virtue. Or her heart.

The thought angered her. And made her all the more determined to take whatever help Blake could give her.

'Blake's offered me a part in one of his movies,' she said brightly, at which Byron's eyes widened considerably.

It crossed Kate's mind that maybe Byron knew of his friend's modus operandi with actresses as well. A momentary concern tightened her chest, but it was quickly dismissed—as quickly as she swallowed the rest of her champagne. The alcohol fizzed down into her near empty stomach— she hadn't eaten much of the formal meal—going straight to her head and giving her some much-needed Dutch courage.

She wasn't by nature a rash person. Or a reckless one. Yet she wanted to be both tonight. She *needed* to be both tonight—needed to throw off her earlier wretchedness, needed to ignore her broken heart and surge boldly and bravely into a new future: a future in which her futile feelings for Lachlan had no role to play.

She had to move on. *Had* to. There was no alternative. Kate was tired of feeling depressed. And of being rejected both personally and professionally. It was time to tap into her acting skills. Time to channel Maddie and just go for it.

'I think, darling Blake,' she said, with a decidedly flirtatious sparkle in her eyes, 'that I am in desperate need of some more dancing.'

Blake almost did a double-take. Even Byron shot him a startled glance. This wasn't the Kate who'd dashed off to the Ladies. This was a different

Kate. A saucier, sexier Kate. Maybe she had more of her sister in her than he'd realised.

In a perverse way, he wasn't sure he liked it. His body did, however, and his erection returned with a vengeance before he'd even taken her into his arms.

Without prompting she slid her own arms up around his neck and pressed herself against him. Blake swore under his breath, knowing she had to be aware of his arousal. It discomfited him, for some reason. As much as he wanted Kate, he had never been the kind of guy who shagged sozzled bridesmaids at weddings, however much they wanted it.

'Sweetheart...' he murmured, noting her over-bright eyes with their dilated pupils. 'How much have you had to drink tonight?'

She blinked up at him, then laughed. 'Not all that much. But I could do with some fresh air. It's rather warm in here. Fancy a walk in the garden? It's lovely down by the water. Not cold at all. We could go and sit in the gazebo whilst you tell me about this wonderful part you have for me.'

Kate knew she was prattling on, but she really wasn't comfortable in the role of vamp, or seductress, or whatever it was she was trying to be. Not that it mattered. Blake already fancied her. She'd felt the evidence more than once. She didn't have to act like this. It wasn't her.

She had no doubt that once they were alone in the gazebo he would make a pass. Kiss her at least.

But what if he wanted to go further than that?

As attractive and sexy as she found him, Kate didn't really want to have sex with Blake tonight. So tacky to act like that at a wedding! Her *sister's* wedding, no less. No, she couldn't throw caution to the wind to that extent. And to go outside with him—to be alone with him in the vast, rather romantically lit grounds—was dangerous in the extreme.

Because she wasn't sure that if he started kissing her she would want him to stop. The way he kept looking at her was powerfully seductive. His hot gaze bored into her like a laser beam, searing her insides and making her want to be even more reckless than she'd vowed to be. She couldn't recall ever feeling quite so...*stirred*.

'Let's go, then,' he said firmly, a possessive

hand on her elbow, steering her towards the exit of the marquee.

Fortunately—or perhaps unfortunately, as it turned out—they were interrupted before they could make their escape. It was her mother, still looking like the very proud mother of the bride, all puffed up and flushed in her very pretty and very expensive pink suit, an older version of Maddie with her bottle blonde hair, but just a little too much make-up for a woman of fifty.

'Maddie sent me to get you, Kate,' Janine Holiday said somewhat breathlessly. 'She wants you to help her change into her going-away outfit.'

'What? So soon? But it's still quite early and—'

'The poor love says she's terribly tired,' Janine cut in. 'As you know, she's been up since the crack of dawn.'

Kate *did* know. She'd been got up as well, and then dragged off to the beauty salon so that she could be plucked and primped and polished until she hardly recognised herself. But she supposed it had been worth it in the end. Blake thought she looked lovely.

Kate didn't believe for a moment that Maddie was 'terribly tired'. That girl was like one of those batteries which never ran down. She knew exactly why Maddie wanted to leave. She'd whispered the reason to Kate earlier. She wanted to have sex with her new husband.

An hour or two ago Kate would have been overwhelmed with jealousy. Now her only feeling was distaste. She might still be in love with Lachlan, but she no longer liked him or wanted him. After what Blake had told her about his cheating behaviour Maddie was welcome to him.

'You'd better go,' Blake said, a wry note in his voice. 'I'll catch you later.'

Kate threw him an apologetic glance before allowing herself to be drawn away by her mother.

'Maddie's already gone upstairs,' Janine said as they headed for the house together. 'I think, Kate, that after she and Lachlan have left your father and I will go home too. I'm pretty tired myself. It's been a long day. Marvellous, but exhausting. What about you?' she added. 'I suppose you won't want to leave that early.'

'No.'

In truth, Kate was horrified at the thought of listening to her parents rave on about Maddie's wedding all the way home. Strathfield was an inner

Western Sydney suburb which was a good half-hour drive from Byron's harbour-side mansion.

'That would be rather rude. The party's only just started. We can't *all* leave early. Besides, Cleo said I could stay the night if I liked, so I think I'll take her up on that offer.'

'Cleo?'

'Byron's wife. You must have met her.'

'I suppose I must have. I've been a bit distracted today. What does she look like?'

'Brunette. Burgundy dress. Very stylish. And very nice. Look, I'll catch a taxi home in the morning. I'll bring the dresses with me when I come.'

'Oh, all right. But perhaps I'd best take Maddie's wedding dress home with me tonight. I wouldn't like anything to happen to it.'

'What on earth could possibly *happen* to it?' Kate asked, amazed and a little hurt.

Janine looked irritated. 'I don't know. I just think it's better to be safe than sorry. Now, off you go. I need to get back to your father before he gets himself into trouble.'

Kate almost laughed. Her father was not the type of man who ever got himself into trouble.

An insurance assessor, he was as conservative as his job, his only passion in life a collection of rare stamps. And, of course, his second and much adored daughter, who'd played Daddy's girl to perfection from the time she was just a tot.

Whenever Maddie perched herself on her father's knee and wrapped her arms around him he could deny her nothing. And he never had. Whatever she wanted, she got. Toys. Clothes. Expensive school excursions. A boob job. And finally, when she turned twenty-one, a car. Which she had promptly wrecked, losing her driving licence as well. This hadn't overly bothered Maddie, because by then she'd always had some obsessed boyfriend very eager to drive her wherever she wanted to go.

Kate trudged up the stairs, sighing as she went. She wished she could hate Maddie. But she didn't. She just couldn't. Yes, her sister was vain, and manipulative, and terribly self-centred. But, despite all that, she was an engaging personality, irrepressible and outgoing, and very, *very* charming. Kate couldn't help admiring her, in a way. And loving her.

More was the pity.

CHAPTER EIGHT

'Oh, THERE YOU ARE!' Maddie exclaimed as Kate walked in.

She'd already taken off her wedding dress and tossed it carelessly onto a nearby chair. She was standing by the bed in nothing but a strapless white lace corset, her double D cup boobs almost spilling over the top. Her stockings and shoes lay in an untidy heap on the floor.

'Join me?' she said as she swept up the bottle of champagne which was sitting in an ice bucket on the bedside table.

Next to it were two flutes, delivered to the room when they'd been getting dressed earlier. Neither of them had felt like drinking at the time. Maddie had been too excited and Kate too wretched.

'For pity's sake, watch what you're doing!' Kate groaned when the cork popped off and champagne started fizzing out of the bottle. Hurrying over, she rescued the precious wedding dress in time, returning it to the plastic cover where it had been residing for the last two weeks.

'Oh, don't be such a worrywart. It's not red wine. Champagne won't even stain. Besides, it's not like I'll be wearing the damned thing ever again. Mum will put it into her treasure box so that she can bring it out and drool over it every now and then. She's got all our grad dresses in there too. Even our christening dresses. Here—have some champers. You might need it.'

'What do you mean, *I* might need it?' Kate asked as she took the glass.

Maddie flashed her one of her mischievous glances. 'Blind Freddie could see that Blake Randall is very taken with you, darls. All thanks to *moi*, of course. If you'd turned up today looking like your usual drack sack he wouldn't be all over you like a rash the way he was on that dance floor a little while ago. Now, does he know you graduated from NIDA?'

'I told him.' Kate took a deep swallow of the cold champagne. 'Your dear husband never even mentioned it to him. Which I find quite odd, since we were supposedly good friends there.'

Maddie laughed. 'Never underestimate the

male ego, darls. Lachlan wouldn't want any of his NIDA buddies stealing his thunder, so to speak. Especially not you, Kate. You're too good an actress. And then there was that other matter...'

'What other matter?'

'Your crush on him,' she stated with bald honesty.

'My *what*?'

Maddie rolled her eyes. 'Please don't pretend you don't know what I'm talking about. It was obvious—even at home. You never stopped talking about him from day one at NIDA. Lachlan tells me it was quite embarrassing...the way you followed him around like a puppy. He said he couldn't even go for coffee without you inviting yourself along.'

Kate could hardly believe what she was hearing. *Lachlan* was the one who had kept inviting *her* for coffee. His wanting to talk to her all the time had been very flattering. It hadn't been just his looks which had made her fall in love with him. But now she saw that he'd just been picking her brain, as most of their conversations had revolved around her acting methods.

A very real fury welled up inside her. Fury plus

a degree of humiliation. How could she have been so taken in by him? But she had. Oh, yes, she *had*.

In her defence, *all* the attractive female students at NIDA had gone ga-ga over him. And most of them had become a girlfriend of Lachlan's at some stage—each of them dated for a while and then dumped, not harshly but cleverly. Lachlan had used buckets of his boyish charm to smooth over each break-up, with the result that they had never had anything bad to say about him, even after he'd moved on.

Kate had waited and waited for him to move on to *her*. She was the only one he hadn't dated, and whilst she knew she couldn't compare with Maddie, she wasn't a total dog. Lots of people said she was quite attractive. But he had never asked her out. Not once.

Just thinking about those wasted years had Kate finishing her first glass of champagne in no time and seeking a refill.

'Oh, come, now,' Kate said as she put the bottle down. 'I wasn't as bad as that. And I wasn't the only girl at NIDA to be impressed. I mean, he is so *very* good-looking. But we all got over that once we realised how up himself he is.'

Kate felt rather proud of her well-delivered lie. Studying acting had come in handy more than once today.

'I certainly don't have a crush on him any more, I can assure you,' she said with a straight face as she lifted the glass to her lips again.

'So you say,' Maddie said, putting down her own glass on a side table and standing with her hands on her hips, eyes narrowed and lips pursed. 'I guess I'd be more inclined to believe you if you had a boyfriend. Look, Lachlan is my husband now, and I don't want to go through my life thinking my sister still has the hots for him. *Do* you?'

Kate drew herself up tall, squared her shoulders and fixed Maddie with uncompromising eyes. 'Now you are being seriously silly. Okay, I admit I did have a small crush on him. Once. But trust me when I say I don't any longer.'

Maddie gave her a long hard glare before shrugging dismissively. 'Well, I'll just have to take your word for it, I suppose. But I did wonder why you seemed so uptight earlier. If I thought that—'

'Maddie, please stop! You've totally got the wrong idea. The reason I was uptight earlier was because I was nervous.'

'Nervous! What about?'

'About being a bridesmaid. I've never been one before.'

'For heaven's sake! I've never been a bride before and *I* wasn't nervous.'

'You're never nervous about anything.'

'True...' Maddie preened. 'Okay, now that's all sorted, let's get back to what I originally wanted to talk to you about. Blake Randall's obvious interest in you...'

'Oh, yes?'

'Yes. Now, I don't want you to waste this opportunity,' Maddie said as she went over to the walk-in wardrobe and came out carrying the very stylish ice-blue woollen dress which her mother had chosen and for which her father had paid a small fortune. 'That's why I said you might need to get a bit tipsy. To give you some Dutch courage,' Maddie added, unzipping the dress and laying it out across the bed. 'Because I *know* you, Kate. You let opportunities go by because you simply won't go for them. So go on—drink up.'

Kate did as she was ordered, glad that the alcohol was already hurrying through her veins and reaching her brain, bringing with it a much-needed devil-may-care attitude.

'You have to have tunnel vision in this world,' Maddie rattled on, stepping into the blue sheath and pulling it up onto her shoulders. 'You can't wait for things to just happen. You have to *make* them happen.'

This was hardly news to Kate. She'd thought exactly the same thing earlier this evening.

'Now, I have a confession to make,' her sister went on, doing up the side zipper and then slipping her bare feet into the pair of nude high heels which were sitting ready for her at the foot of the bed. 'When you brought Lachlan home last Christmas even though I'd almost decided to marry Riley I knew I didn't love him. But I liked him, and I knew he'd give me a good life money-wise. He owns his own plumbing business and everyone knows that plumbers earn heaps. But then I took one look at Lachlan and saw an opportunity for a much better life—a life which would be very exciting and very glamorous, with a husband who was gorgeous and brilliant and seriously sexy. I realised suddenly that I couldn't settle for Riley, even though he was very good in bed. I wanted more. I wanted Lachlan and what he could give me. I mean, the temptation to go for him was overwhelming.'

She hesitated briefly and sent Kate an apologetic glance.

'I know you liked him, Kate, and I'm sorry. I dare say you were hurt when we left together that day. But I simply had to try to get him to fall in love with me. And he already wanted me, don't you see? He didn't want you. You weren't his type.'

'Yes, I'd already gathered that,' Kate said, thankful now that she was becoming, if not merry, decidedly numb. Without thinking she lifted the glass to her lips and took another deep swallow.

'So…you're not in love with Lachlan either, then?' Kate said, trying not to look and sound as shocked as she was.

'Love?' Maddie scoffed, smoothing down her skirt before walking over and picking up her champagne once more. 'What's love?' she said dismissively after a sip. 'A very temporary state— especially where the male sex is concerned. Their idea of love is usually all about sex. A woman has about eighteen months at best to get what she wants from a man before he goes off the boil. If you want marriage then you have to get him to propose during the first twelve months. I'm under no illusions. I know that Lachlan will stray. He's too handsome and sexy to stay faithful—especially in the movie world. But I'll always be his wife—or at least his very rich *ex*-wife.'

Kate was appalled. And suddenly she must have looked it.

'Don't get me wrong,' Maddie went on as she stepped over to the dressing table to attend to her make-up and hair. 'I *do* care for Lachlan. Very much. And we have great chemistry in bed. I couldn't stand to marry a man who wasn't a good lover. Makes up for a lot of things…great sex. It also makes a man amenable to doing what *you* want. Which brings me back to my advice to you about Blake Randall,' she said, turning round to look straight at Kate as she sprayed herself liberally with perfume.

'And what advice would that be?' Kate asked. Her emotions were still outwardly under control, but inside she was dissolving. Maddie didn't even *love* Lachlan. All she wanted was the good life. *Dear God…*

'Get him into the sack ASAP. Don't wait. He'll be off back to Hollywood in a few days. Strike while the iron is hot. And his iron *is* hot. For *you*, darls. Lachlan says he's a sucker when it comes to pretty young actresses. And you *do* look pretty tonight, Kate. More than pretty. I actually feel a little jealous.'

Kate had to laugh. 'Now, *that's* not true,' she said, turning to fill her glass again. How had it become empty so quickly? 'You've never been jealous of me.'

'Oh, I wouldn't say that. I envy your acting ability. It's brilliant.'

And so is yours, Kate thought with a touch of malice.

'Blake Randall is going to get a real shock once he realises how good you are,' Maddie went on. 'But he won't ever realise that unless you keep him around long enough to see it.'

'Maddie, he's already offered me a part in one of his movies,' she stated, bypassing her distress and surrendering to irritation. 'I don't *have* to sleep with him.'

'Oh, God—don't be so naive.'

'I'm *not* naive.'

'Yes, you are. Hopelessly. It's a man's world, Kate. They have all the power. Our only power comes from sex. I found that out years ago. Now, how do I look?'

Kate sighed. 'Like you always do. Gorgeous.'

'Thanks, darls. I love you—you know that, don't you?'

Kate did know that—which was perverse. Somehow she smiled and came forward to give her sister a hug. 'I hope you'll be very happy,' she said, and tried to mean it.

'Oh, I will be. I know it. Now, where did I put my bouquet...?'

CHAPTER NINE

BLAKE WATCHED FROM the sidelines as the beaming couple said their goodbyes, the bride making a big fuss over her parents before throwing her bouquet straight at her sister.

Kate laughed, but the laughter didn't touch her eyes. Blake still wasn't sure what was going on in that girl's head. She'd come back downstairs shortly after the bride, sipping a full glass of champagne as she made her way a bit shakily down the steps, her spare hand gripping the banister for support. She'd looked lost and decidedly tipsy.

Blake would have gone to her then if Cleo hadn't suddenly appeared by his side, striking up a conversation and leaving Blake no opportunity to do anything except surreptitiously watch Kate's rather unsteady progress.

Once at the bottom of the stairs Kate had scanned the crowd of guests for a few seconds, then walked over to stand with her back against a nearby wall, her lips no longer sipping but drinking fast.

Fortunately by the time the bride threw her bouquet her glass was almost empty, otherwise champagne might have gone everywhere. Despite acting as if she was thrilled, Blake suspected she was on the verge of tears—which sent him striding over to her side, where he slid a firm arm around her waist and pulled her against him.

'I think you've had way too much to drink,' he murmured.

'*I* don't,' she said, lifting big brown eyes up to his.

They were very glassy, but still very lovely.

'I don't think I've had *nearly* enough. Let's go and find another bottle of this delicious champagne.'

'Not right now, darling heart. Let's go for that walk down to the gazebo instead. Get you some much-needed fresh air first.'

'Whatever you say,' she said, with a nonchalant shrug of her slender shoulders. 'Just wait while I give this bouquet to my mother. She might want to take it home with her…have it cast in gold.'

Blake smiled at the unexpected sarcasm. Or was it jealousy? Was *that* what her changeable moods tonight had been all about? Jealousy over her sister?

He was tempted to ask her, but then decided best not. He didn't want to start talking about Maddie. He wanted to talk about *her*. Kate. The deliciously sexy and intriguing Kate.

If only she'd realise that not every man liked the obvious. *He* certainly didn't. He couldn't wait to take her to dinner tomorrow night, and to get her by herself afterwards in a romantic setting befitting their first time together. He'd already asked Byron if he could use his city penthouse for the next few days. It was a fantastically glamorous pad and Kate would be suitably impressed.

And Blake wanted to impress her. Impress her and protect her and make her happy—which he could do by giving her career a leg-up and getting his leg over at the same time. It wasn't as though she wouldn't enjoy sex with him. It certainly wouldn't be a case of her just lying back and thinking of her career. Blake *knew* he was a good lover. Always had been.

God, you're an arrogant devil, Blake conceded

inwardly. *Has it even crossed your mind that she might say no to you? The bed part, that is, not the movie part?*

It was a novel thought, but not one he took seriously. Kate wouldn't say no to him. He'd seen the desire in her eyes on the dance floor earlier—felt it in her deliciously uptight body. It was just a matter of finding the right place and the right time. And making the right moves, of course.

Blake had every confidence that nothing would come between him and success.

A wave of relief flooded Kate after they'd all left—Maddie and Lachlan first, and then her parents, her mother taking with her Maddie's wedding dress and veil. Kate certainly didn't want to be responsible for them, or even to see them ever again. Thank God she'd handed over the bouquet as well, or she just might have thrown it into the harbour.

In truth, her broken heart had lightened considerably with their departure. Out of sight was out of mind. To a degree. Of course it helped that she was just a little bit drunk. No, a long way drunk, she accepted with an uncharacteristically naughty giggle. It helped her be able to return to the seriously attractive man who clearly wanted *her*—Kate Holiday. Not her blonde bombshell sister. *Her.*

God, she adored the way Blake looked at her. So hot and so hungry. It made her feel weak at the knees, and yet perversely powerful at the same time. She smiled flirtatiously as she walked slowly back to him, unconsciously acting the vamp, swinging her hips and licking her suddenly dry lips.

Bloody hell, thought Blake, his body leaping into action. If she didn't watch it they'd be taking things a lot further down in the gazebo. Only her obviously drunken state would stop him. But, damn it all, resisting her was going to be difficult.

Keep the touching to a minimum, then, he warned himself. *And definitely no kissing. In fact it would be much better if you went back into the marquee and just danced*, he told himself.

Yes, and perhaps get her some more champagne. Give her something to do with that mouth of hers instead of doing what she was doing.

Actually she didn't wait for him to do anything—just came up very close, slid her arms up around his neck, right then and there, and planted those tempting lips right on his.

What was a red-blooded male supposed to do? One with a hard-on the size of Nelson's column?

Without thinking it through he kissed her back for a few seconds before common sense returned. Then, taking her firmly by the hips, he eased her away and speared her with a reproachful look.

'Naughty, Kate,' he murmured, aware of other people staring at them. 'Come on—we're off to the gazebo. And we'll pick up a bottle of champagne on the way.'

Kate giggled. She liked being called naughty. Liked *being* naughty. God, but he was a good kisser. She couldn't wait for him to kiss her some more. For longer next time. She'd only briefly felt the tip of his tongue. She wanted more of it, diving in deeper, making her head swirl again. She wanted...

Oh, she didn't know what she wanted. Oblivion, she supposed. Oblivion from the horrid thoughts which kept jumping into her head.

Maddie doesn't love Lachlan...

Lachlan doesn't want you...he wants Maddie... You're not his type...

She needed to block those thoughts out—needed to replace them with wild, wonderful thoughts; needed to have this man's arms around her again. Not just on the dance floor, or during a brief kiss, but all night. In bed.

Kate grabbed Blake's hand and squeezed it tight. 'I do *so* like you,' she said.

He smiled down at her. 'Good.'

It was cold down in the gazebo, a sea breeze having sprung up. When Kate shivered Blake took off his jacket and draped it round her shoulders.

'Such a gentleman,' she said, appreciating the warmth.

'Not always.'

'Oh. You forgot to get some more champagne.'

'You've had enough.'

'Don't be such a spoilsport.'

'I'm just protecting your virtue.'

She laughed. 'I'm not a virgin.'

'I should hope not. But what's that got to do with protecting your virtue?'

'Maybe I don't *want* you to protect me. Maybe I want you to ravage me senseless,' she said, a wild glint flashing in her eyes. 'Not here, of course. I understand we can't do it here. It's cold and uncomfortable. But I'm staying the night at Byron's house. Are you?'

'Yes...' he said.

Kate ignored his frown. 'In that case we could spend the night together. In *your* room, preferably,' she added, knowing the other bedroom would still smell of Maddie's perfume.

Blake knew they were getting into dangerous waters here. The alcohol was making her reckless. The really dangerous part was that he rather *liked* reckless. Yet he knew being reckless wasn't in Kate's true nature. She was going to regret this in the morning.

But, hell on earth... He was only human. And a long way from being a saint.

'Kate,' he said, clutching at what conscience he *did* have where women and sex were concerned. 'I can't. I'm sorry. You're drunk.'

She stared at him, shock and confusion in her eyes. 'What? You don't *ever* go to bed with a woman who's had a few glasses of champagne?

I find that hard to believe. From what I've heard you're the very *devil* with women.'

'Not always,' he returned. 'It depends on the woman.'

Tears suddenly filled her eyes. Tears and a type of rage. 'The truth is you don't really want me, do you? Not enough. I thought you did. I thought... Oh, what does it matter *what* I thought?' she cried, jumping up and throwing his jacket at him. 'You're a total bastard and I hate you!'

CHAPTER TEN

BLAKE STOOD OUTSIDE the bedroom door, listening to the sound of Kate sobbing inside. Cleo crossed her arms and glared at him, having joined the chase when she'd spotted Blake racing after a fleeing Kate. Both of them had followed her back into the house and up the staircase, unable to catch her before she'd slammed the bedroom door in their faces.

'What on earth did you do to her?' Cleo demanded. 'You were both getting along fine earlier in the evening. She was glued to you when you were dancing, and then later you were kissing down in the foyer.'

'We went for a walk to the gazebo,' he said, sighing.

'And?'

'I refused to have sex with her.'

'*What?* Good Lord—that's a new one.'

'Look, she was drunk. I don't have sex with seriously intoxicated women, no matter how much I fancy them.'

'That's very commendable of you, Blake. But I'm not sure if I totally believe you. You *do* have a rather ruthless reputation where the ladies are concerned, you know.'

'No, I *don't* know,' Blake snapped. 'Just because I enjoy a bachelor lifestyle it doesn't mean I treat women badly.'

He supposed his so-called reputation was a hangover from those few months after Claudia had left him, when he had indulged in some thoughtless revenge sex. With actresses, of course. But those days were long gone. Okay, so his girlfriends were still usually actresses, or people involved in the movie industry. But that was only logical. Who else did he meet?

'Fair enough,' Cleo said. 'Don't get angry with *me*. I'm just telling you what I've heard on the grapevine. Obviously Kate has heard something similar. Still, it was a strange reaction on her part. I would have thought she'd be impressed by your gallantry.'

'Obviously not. I don't understand her, Cleo.'

'I think you should go in there and talk to her.'

'She'll probably scream at me to get out.'

'If you really like her, you have to try. Don't wait. Waiting never works where women are concerned.'

'You're right.' He tried the doorknob and found it wasn't locked. Still, he hesitated.

'I really must get back to the party,' Cleo said. 'Byron will wonder where I've got to.'

'Tell him you had to check on the baby.'

'He won't believe that. April's at her godmother's tonight.'

'Well, say you had to call and check that she was okay.'

Cleo laughed. 'I can see you're an accomplished liar.'

'Hardly. I'm usually accused of being brutally honest.'

'That's not always a virtue, Blake—especially when it comes to women. Kindness is what we value most in a man, which might involve the occasional white lie. Anyway, I must go. I'll catch up with you later and see what you achieved.'

She was gone in a flash, leaving Blake mulling over what she'd said about kindness.

I can be kind, he told himself as he slowly

turned the knob. *Can't I? Yes, of course I can.* And he pushed open the door.

Kate was lying face down on the bed, weeping into a mountain of pillows.

'Kate?' he said gently as he approached the bed.

'Go away,' she blubbered. 'Leave me alone.'

He ignored that and sat down on the side of the bed. 'Not until you tell me what I did that was so wrong.'

'You don't understand,' she cried in muffled tones.

'No, I don't. Not unless you tell me.'

She rolled over and showed him her pitiful face, her flushed cheeks stained with mascara and tears, her eyes swollen with weeping. 'I… I can't,' she blurted out. 'It's too…humiliating.'

'Kate, I like you. A lot. And I fancy you. A lot. I have every intention of making love to you tomorrow night, after I've taken you out for a suitably romantic dinner and then taken you back to a suitably romantic place, befitting what a lovely girl like you deserves. Does that sound like I don't really want you?'

She shook her head from side to side, then buried her face in her hands. 'It's nothing to do with you, really.'

'Then what's it to do with?'

'I can't tell you.'

Blake took her hands away from her face and held them, forcing her to look up into his eyes. 'It's something to do with your sister, isn't it?'

Her puffy eyes widened.

'I'm a fairly observant character,' he went on. 'I noticed that every time you had something to do with your sister today you became upset. Unhappy. Different. When you came downstairs after helping Maddie with her going-away outfit you were *very* different. I couldn't put my finger on it at the time, but in hindsight I think you were extremely upset and that you tried to hide your feelings behind a rather reckless façade. As much as I hate to admit it, I don't think you really *wanted* to have sex with me. Not me personally. You were just craving distraction. That's why you drank so much as well—to dull whatever pain it was that your sister caused you.'

He stopped talking then, and she just stared at him, her expression bewildered at first, and then just bleak. 'If I tell you, you're going to think me a fool.'

'I doubt that very much. We're all capable of foolishness. So what is it, Kate? What's been bothering you so much today?'

She blinked, then sighed, and then shook her head again. 'I can't believe I'm going to tell you this. I… I never wanted to tell anyone—never wanted anyone to know, especially my family.'

'Well, I'm not family. Sometimes it's good to tell outsiders. They can give you objective advice.'

Though, damn it all, he wasn't feeling all that objective where Kate was concerned. She touched him as he had not been touched in years.

'Just blurt it out,' he insisted. 'Stop thinking about what I might think of you and tell me this awful truth, whatever it is.'

Her face filled with anguish. 'That's very easy to say. Not so easy to do.'

'Just *do* it, Kate.'

She sighed again—a heavy but resigned sigh. 'All right, I will. The thing is…the awful truth is…that I'm in love with Lachlan.' And she hung her head in a gesture of shame. Or possibly humiliation.

Blake supposed later that he should not have been so shocked. After all, practically every female who'd seen one of Lachlan's movies was in love with him. Young. Old. Married. Single. They all adored him. That was why his romantic comedies were so successful.

'I see,' he bit out, angry with her at first, for being so stupid as to fall in love with someone so shallow, and then sympathetic—because hadn't he done exactly the same thing at her age? He'd fallen in love with Claudia, who was probably even worse than Lachlan.

'You *don't* see,' she cried, sitting up and wringing her hands together. 'And you *do* think I'm a fool.'

'No,' he returned slowly. 'I don't think that at all. I can understand why you might have fallen in love with him. He's very good-looking, and extremely charming when he needs to be. So how long have you been in love with Lachlan?'

'What? Oh, since the first day we went to NIDA together.'

'Love at first sight, then?' Blake said, thinking

it was more like lust at first sight. Even *he* hadn't fallen in love with Claudia at first sight.

Blake had always been a bit of a cynic where true love was concerned. Claudia had had to work hard on him in order to convince him of her love. And she had—convinced him, that was—which had made the speed of her betrayal after their marriage all the more devastating.

'Yes,' she said sadly. 'But he didn't ever return my feelings. He liked me okay, so I thought I was in with a chance—especially when he was between girlfriends. He was always nice to me... often seeking me out to help him with assignments. But Maddie told me tonight that he found my crush on him quite embarrassing. That's what he called it. A crush...' Her laugh was slightly hysterical, her hands still twisting in her lap.

'And when exactly did she tell you this?' Blake asked gently.

'Oh, when I came up here tonight to help her change. Though she didn't really want my help. She just wanted reassurance that I was over my crush and that I didn't still have the hots for her precious husband. Which I assured her I didn't.

After that she proceeded to give me a lecture about you.'

'About *me*?'

'Yes, she advised me to sleep with you. Said it would be good for my career.'

'Which advice you followed to a T,' he said ruefully.

Her face twisted. 'No—no, you've got it all wrong. My coming on to you wasn't about my career. It was because you seemed genuinely attracted to me and I was flattered...especially after what Maddie said about Lachlan wanting her and never wanting me. Apparently I simply wasn't his type. So I thought...well... I must be Blake's type. So when I came downstairs and saw you, waiting for me and smiling at me, it made me feel a bit better. Then, when I kissed you, I felt a lot better. Yes, I know I'm drunk, but I needed you, Blake. Needed to feel desirable. I wanted to be wanted. By someone. *Anyone!* So when you turned me down I just felt so bad. I... I couldn't handle it.'

Blake watched as her already fragile control began to shatter.

'And the worst thing is,' she added, her eyes filling with the most heartbreaking distress, 'she doesn't even love him. Not really. Of course she's sexually attracted to him. Who isn't? But the reason she married him was to live the good life—whatever that is. Oh, God...'

Kate couldn't go on, feeling a tight ball of emotion gather in her chest as all the hurt, misery and frustration of this past year overwhelmed her. A cry such as she'd never heard before punched from her lungs. It sounded like a wounded animal—a wounded *dying* animal.

She froze, her shoulders stiffening with the effort to hold on to herself, her eyes wide with shock. But it was no use. There was no stopping the avalanche of pain once it broke free. Whirling away from Blake's startled face, she threw herself back onto the pillows and let go, sobbing her heart out with even more fervour than she had earlier.

It was horrible, humiliating, but she had nothing left of control or courage. She told herself that she didn't even care that Blake was witnessing her breakdown.

It was odd, then, that underneath her almost hysterical weeping, plus her dizzy and decidedly alcohol-infused thoughts, she had enough brainpower left to worry that he probably wouldn't want her in one of his movies now—let alone anything else. It bothered her greatly that he would see her for what she was. A stupid fool and a total failure!

CHAPTER ELEVEN

BLAKE WAS USED to women's tears. Good actresses could summon them up at the drop of a hat. But these weren't just ordinary tears. Kate was sobbing like nothing he'd heard before. If she kept this up she would make herself ill.

He wondered if he should go and find Cleo and Byron—get them to call a doctor, someone who could give Kate something to calm her down. Though Lord knew the possibility of getting a doctor to make a house call at this hour on a Saturday night was highly unlikely. Perhaps they might have something in their medicine cabinet which would be useful. A tranquilliser of some sort.

Whilst he mulled over this possible solution he tried placing his hand on the back of her head and stroking her long hair, murmuring the sort of soft, soothing words which he often put into a script but had never actually said before.

'Now, now—don't cry...there, there...'

How soft her hair was. How silky and soft and sexy.

Must not think about sex now, he told himself sternly. *Time to be kind. Time to just be a good friend.* Clearly Kate needed a good friend—someone who would comfort her and then talk sense to her, when she was capable of listening. Which probably wouldn't be tonight.

But still... Fancy falling in love with Lachlan! What a total waste of time *that* was. It probably wasn't true love, either. Just an infatuation. He was the kind of guy girls got infatuated with very easily. His golden boy looks, of course, and that brilliant smile, that overpowering charm.

How ironic that Kate's sister didn't really love him—that she'd just married him for the good life. Not that she didn't put on a good act. She played the besotted bride to perfection. And she had the looks to carry off the role. She might even make the marriage a success. After all, if she didn't love him she'd probably be prepared to tolerate his infidelities. Either that or she herself might move on to someone even more successful, the way Claudia had.

Claudia...

Blake thought of Claudia as he stroked Kate's hair. What a bitch! A selfish, ambitious, cold-blooded bitch. He'd always hoped she'd fall flat on her face once she'd dumped him for that aging Hollywood producer. But she hadn't. Her career—whilst not top drawer—had been very successful.

She was now married to one of the executives at Unicorn Pictures. Blake had run into her at a party not that long ago, and she'd been sickeningly nice to him. Admittedly, he'd been sickeningly nice back—even chatting away very amicably with her reasonably handsome and annoyingly clever husband. No point in making enemies in Hollywood. Not good for business.

Quite frankly, he was well and truly over her. A good feeling, that, after spending years being bitter and somewhat cynical—especially where aspiring young actresses were concerned.

The fact that Kate was an aspiring young actress did not escape Blake, but she wasn't like any aspiring young actress he'd ever met before. Besides, he was *glad* she was exactly that. It gave him the opportunity to get to know her better and to do what he'd been aching to do all night.

Stop thinking about sex!

Blake gritted his teeth and continued stroking her hair, valiantly ignoring his very active hormones and concentrating on giving Kate what she needed at that moment. Which was gentle words and a soft touch.

Hopefully by tomorrow night her needs would be different. It didn't escape Blake that she'd had a very mixed agenda when she'd offered herself to him in the gazebo. No doubt there was some rebound and revenge in there somewhere. But he still felt confident that she was genuinely attracted to him. He knew she hadn't faked that kiss.

Finally the sobbing subsided into the occasional shudder, and Blake's hand fell away when Kate abruptly rolled over.

'I... I have to go to the bathroom,' she choked out, scrambling off the bed and dashing for the nearby en-suite.

Blake groaned when he heard the sound of Kate throwing up, torn between offering further help and keeping a compassionate distance. In the end he decided on compassionate distance. He heard her flush the toilet a couple of times, then turn on a tap. Possibly to rinse out her mouth. He heard the tap snapped off but she didn't emerge. He heard her mutter something under her breath, followed by a sigh and some rustling sounds.

When a few minutes had passed and all had fallen ominously silent in the bathroom he made his way reluctantly over to the shut door. His hand had actually lifted to knock when the door opened.

Blake sucked in a breath sharply. *Bloody hell!*

She wasn't naked. But she'd removed her bridesmaid's dress and was standing there dressed in a strapless black satin corset which was so sexy it was criminal—especially when worn with flesh-coloured stay-up stockings and high heels.

'I had to take my dress off,' she explained shakily, looking both sheepish and embarrassed. 'I got some vomit on it. Mum's going to be furious with me,' she added, wincing. 'I… I would have had a shower, but I didn't know I was going to stay here overnight and I didn't bring any nightwear with me. I'm not trying to be provocative. Truly.'

She swayed on her high heels, grabbing the doorknob as if her life depended on it.

'Oh, God, will someone please stop the room from spinning around?'

Blake took a firm hold of her and led her back over to the bed, sitting her down and doing his level best to keep his male mind from corrupting his good intentions.

Kate didn't need him ogling her. But her body was exactly the kind of body he admired on a woman—tall and slender, but with enough curves to be unmistakably feminine. Still, he already knew that—had thought it when he'd first seen her walking down the staircase. She had great skin too. Clear and almost translucent, indicating that her honey-gold hair was probably natural and not the result of hours of painstaking dyeing.

'What you need,' he said gently as he removed her shoes and then her stockings, without once looking at the V between her thighs or her tiny waist…or her very nice cleavage, 'is a big drink of water followed by a good night's sleep.'

'I did drink some water in the bathroom,' she told him.

'And you kept it down?'

'Yes.'

'Good. Now, into bed with you.'

Again without really looking at her, he pulled the bedclothes back and angled her in between the sheets before swiftly covering her, right up to her neck.

But just when he thought he could safely make his escape her head lifted from the pillow, the bedcovers slipping a little—*darn it*.

Her puffy eyes sought his, their expression plaintive. 'Please don't go. Not 'til I've fallen asleep.'

'Oh, but I…um…'

'I won't jump on you, I promise.'

His smile was wry. *What a shame.* He wouldn't mind one bit if she did. Like they said, the road to hell was paved with good intentions.

'Very well,' he agreed, and lay down next to her. On top of the quilt, not under it.

She rolled over and stared at him with wonder in her sleepy eyes. 'You're really a very nice man,' she murmured. 'Very…kind.'

'There are a lot of people who would disagree with you.'

'Then they don't know the real you.' She yawned. 'They say men should be judged by their actions, not their words. You're a gentleman, no matter what other people might think.'

Blake wondered exactly what 'other people' she was talking about. Was his reputation with women really that bad? Then he wondered what she'd think of him tomorrow night, when he took her to dinner and set out to seduce her with every weapon he had in his considerable arsenal.

He rolled over and looked her straight in her heavy-lidded eyes. 'You should go to sleep now,' he advised. 'You're going to have a seriously late night tomorrow.'

'Am I?'

Was that a quiver of excitement in her voice?

Blake gave in to temptation and bent forward to kiss her—not on the lips, but on her slightly clammy forehead. 'You'd better believe it, sweetheart. We have a dinner date, remember?'

'Oh, yes,' was all she said, with what sounded like a satisfied sigh.

'Roll over the other way,' he advised thickly. 'I'll stroke your hair until you drop off.'

She obeyed him, sighing again when he started stroking.

Touching her—even her hair—was agony. But he did it, thinking all the while that she was worth the effort.

It was a relief when she fell asleep and he could creep out of the room, telling himself all the while that he wouldn't have to wait too long before he could satisfy the lust she kept on evoking in him. Less than twenty-four hours.

But as he stood in the doorway and glanced back at her it crossed Blake's testosterone-fired brain that once the alcohol was out of Kate's system and she didn't have to watch the man she loved marry her sister she might not be quite the same person who'd thrown herself at him tonight. Tomorrow morning she might be filled with shame and embarrassment. She might actually say no to him.

What a horrific thought!

Blake closed the door and walked slowly towards the staircase, pondering such a possibility. Not for long, however. Confidence in his own abilities had never been a problem for Blake. He had always achieved what he'd set his sights on. And he'd set his sights on getting Kate into his bed.

She wouldn't say no to him. He'd make sure of that!

CHAPTER TWELVE

'IT'S GOOD OF you to drive me home,' Kate said with stiff politeness once they were out of Byron's driveway.

Blake glanced over at her from behind the wheel of his borrowed Lexus. She looked vastly different from the glamorous bridesmaid of last night. Just a simple girl this morning, wearing dark jeans, trainers, and a grey sweatshirt which had a picture of the Opera House on it. No make-up, and her damp and very straight hair pulled back into a ponytail, not a curl or a wave in sight. Not a hint of perfume, either.

Blake wondered if this was some ploy to get him to lose interest in her. Fat chance of that happening. He'd thought of little else all night. Besides, he adored the way she looked. So natural, yet still so sexy.

'My pleasure,' he replied warmly.

She didn't say anything further, gazing out of

the passenger window like some tourist taking in the sights. Blake doubted it was anything like that. He suspected, as he'd feared, that she'd woken this morning feeling pretty bad about what had happened the night before.

Cleo had taken a breakfast tray up to her room around ten, reporting back that Kate seemed somewhat subdued.

'There's no need to feel embarrassed,' he said at last.

Her head whipped round and her expression was totally devoid of embarrassment. Or distress. 'I'm not,' she denied. 'I was for a short while this morning. But not any longer.'

'Good.'

'I know I made a fool of myself last night, but that's all in the past now. I have to move on.'

'You definitely do.'

'I dare say that sooner or later I'll get over being in love with Lachlan, but until that happens I'm not going to waste any more of my life mooning over him or wishing things were different. I'm going to concentrate on my career—one hundred and ten percent.'

'Atta girl.'

She threw him a droll glance. 'That doesn't mean I'm going to jump into bed with *you*, just because you've offered me a part in one of your movies.'

Blake almost ran into the back of the car in front of him, braking just in time. He hadn't noticed that the lights ahead had turned red, bringing the traffic to an abrupt halt. As, it seemed, were his plans for tonight.

'Are you saying that your being attracted to me last night was all about the drink, then?' he asked casually. Oh, *so* casually. If there was one thing Blake had learned about the female sex since the debacle with Claudia, it was never to let a girl know you wanted her like crazy.

Kate scrunched up her face. 'I didn't think so at the time. But in hindsight I suppose it did play a part. Look, I want to be strictly honest with you, Blake. I was in a pathetic state last light. Your attention flattered my rather fragile self-esteem. You're a good-looking man. You're also power- ful and successful. I'm not used to men like you coming on to me.'

'Then more fool them,' he said, and smiled over at her.

She didn't smile back. 'Please don't,' she bit out.

'Don't what?'

'Don't keep flattering me. I don't appreciate it. Now, I have a couple of questions to ask you about this part you've offered me. Unless, of course, you've changed your mind about that now you've seen how I usually look,' she added with a steely glance his way.

Brother, that 'fragile self-esteem' of hers seemed to have taken a back seat. There was not a hint of vulnerability in her eyes at this moment. Kate had suddenly turned into one tough cookie. Blake suppressed a smile. He liked her tough almost as much as he liked her tipsy.

The lights turned green and he drove on. More slowly this time.

'I actually like the way you look today,' he told her. 'I'm not into Barbie dolls. So the offer still stands. It would be a wonderful addition to your résumé and will get you more work. Not here in Australia, however. You'd have to move to LA and get yourself an American agent.'

'Move to LA!' she exclaimed, her eyes widening for a split second before she got control of herself again. 'I didn't realise— I…um…forgot you'd moved over there.'

'I'll probably make the occasional movie back here in Australia, but not the one I'm offering you. Look, we don't actually start shooting until late November, so you've got plenty of time to get yourself organised and over there. We're still in pre-production and I've a few more minor characters to cast.'

'I see,' she said thoughtfully. 'And how will you go about doing that?'

Blake shrugged. 'I'll have a couple of the casting agencies I use send me some likely candidates and I'll give them all an audition. Then I'll choose.'

'In that case that's what I want to do too,' Kate said firmly. 'Go for a proper audition up against other people.'

Blake suppressed his frustration and kept his voice calm. 'But, Kate, there's no need. The role's yours.'

'Why? It doesn't make sense. Unless what Lachlan said was true. That you give the girls you fancy small roles in your movies just so you can shag them every night.'

'Lachlan said *what*?'

'You heard me.'

'Bastard.'

'Is it true?' she demanded. '*Do* you do that?'

Bloody hell. What did he say to that?

'I have done,' he admitted reluctantly. 'Once or twice. In the long-distant past when I was hurting after Claudia divorced me. I'm not proud of it, but I haven't done anything like that for many years. I can't understand why Lachlan would say such a thing. These days I would never risk the success of one of my movies by offering actresses roles on the strength of how much I fancy them.'

'That's what Lachlan said too. That's why you only ever offer the girls you fancy really *small* roles.'

Blake's temper rose. 'So when did Lachlan say all this to you?' he demanded through clenched teeth.

'Last night.'

'Yes, of course. It *would* have been last night. *When*, exactly, last night?'

'When I left you briefly to go to the Ladies. He followed me. He said he cared about me and was worried about me getting tangled up with you.'

'Yeah. Right. And you believed him?'

'I believed what he said about *you*. After all, you'd already offered me a small part in one of your movies without knowing if I could act or not.'

'Firstly, madam, I *do* know you can act. You're a graduate of NIDA, for heaven's sake! Secondly, it is *not* a small role. It's a very good supporting role. Thirdly, I didn't offer you the role because I wanted to "shag" you,' he insisted. 'God, I hate that term. It sounds disgusting. I much prefer to say "have sex", or "sleep with", or even "make love". Anyway, wanting to have sex with you isn't the reason I offered you that job.'

'Oh? What was, then?' Both her question and her eyes were full of scepticism.

Blake sighed. 'I just wanted to make you happy. To make you smile.'

She stared at him for a long moment. 'So you offered me a job out of pity?' she bit out, angry now.

'Absolutely not! I'm not into pity—especially where my movies are concerned.'

'What *are* you into, then?' she asked, a challenging note in her voice.

'Success. And satisfaction.'

'What kind of satisfaction?'

His smile was rueful. 'What do you want me to say, Kate? Okay, so I want to have sex with you. That's hardly a hanging offence. I'm single. You're single. You haven't got a boyfriend and you're not a virgin. I assume you *do* have a sex life? I honestly thought you might enjoy going to bed with me. I'd certainly enjoy going to bed with you. But, aside from all that, I wasn't lying when I said my main motivation for all the things I did last night was to put a smile on your face. That was God's honest truth and it still is. I'm sorry if I've offended you. That was the last thing I wanted to do. Look, if it makes you happy I'll give you a proper screen test for the role. We can do it tonight. I'm sure I've already told you that I'm staying in Byron's city penthouse for the next couple of days. We could go there early this evening, before I take you out to dinner. Or are you reneging on that as well?'

'I'm not reneging on anything. I just need to get some things sorted in my head.'

'Such as what?'

'Such as if my audition's all right, and you still offer me the role, does the offer come with strings attached? Will you expect me to sleep with you at some stage?'

He looked at her long and hard. 'Only if you want to,' he said.

She didn't answer straight away, just turned her head to stare out through the passenger window for a while before glancing back at him.

'Fair enough,' she said, and rewarded him with a small, rather enigmatic smile.

He wondered what it meant, that smile. Whatever, he took some comfort from it. And some confidence. Which was strange, given that confidence was never usually a problem with him—especially with members of the opposite sex.

But Kate rattled him in ways he had yet to fully understand. Blake knew he was very attracted to her, but she stirred other emotions in him besides lust—emotions that were both uncharacteristic and unfamiliar.

In the past few years his relationships with women had basically been selfish ones, his only concern what pleasure they could bring to his life. Sex. Companionship. Compliments.

Oh, yes, he enjoyed the way the women in his world flirted with him, and flattered him, and, yes, were only too willing to go to bed with him. Which suited Blake just fine. He never felt he had to bend over backwards to please them. Didn't need to declare love or promise commitment to enjoy their company.

Kate, however, brought out the gentleman in him. Yes, he wanted her—but not quite so selfishly. His tendency to think only of himself was tempered by a compulsion to try to make everything right in her world. To make her... Yes...to make her *happy*. Of course that didn't mean he wouldn't try to seduce her tonight. He would. But he would stop if she made it clear that she didn't want him to. The trick was to make sure she *did* want him to...

'You might have to make a slight detour,' she said suddenly. 'I'd like to drop off my bridesmaid dress at the dry cleaner's. No way am I taking it home the way it is. Do you know your way to the big shopping centre at Burwood?'

'Not exactly.' He wasn't as familiar with the western suburbs as he was with the eastern, having being brought up there.

'We're not far away now. I'll give you directions, if you like.'

Half an hour later they were back in the Lexus and heading for Strathfield, which was the next suburb going west.

'It will do you good to move away from home,' Blake said, after seeing how stressed Kate had been at the dry cleaner's, despite the lady there assuring her that the dress would be as good as new once cleaned properly. 'Your mother sounds like a pain. And it's perfectly obvious that Maddie is the family pet.'

Kate sighed. 'You're right on both those counts.'

'Then why are you finding excuses not to come to Hollywood and make a new life for yourself? You said you wanted to move on. So do it!'

'I'm not making excuses. I just want to make it on my own. I don't want charity.'

Lord, but she was one difficult girl. Any other actress would have jumped at the chance.

'Don't you believe in your acting ability?' he challenged.

Her chin came up and her eyes flashed. 'Yes, I do. I'm very good. *Damned* good, actually.'

'Then be "damned good" tonight and you'll be on your way to LA.'

CHAPTER THIRTEEN

'WHERE'S YOUR BRIDESMAID DRESS?' were her mother's first words when Kate walked into the family kitchen shortly after midday. 'Don't tell me it's stuffed into that silly little bag!'

Kate counted to ten, then said, 'It's at the dry cleaner's. Someone knocked into me and I spilt some wine on it.'

'Oh, for pity's sake, Kate. Couldn't you have been more careful? Just as well I brought Maddie's dress home with me or that would probably be ruined too.'

'My dress is not ruined,' Kate countered, quite calmly, hugging the hope that soon she wouldn't have to put up with this kind of thing. 'The dry cleaner said it would be as good as new.'

'I hope so. Did Maddie finally get you? She rang me from the airport and said she'd tried to ring you but your phone was turned off.'

'Yes. Yes, it was.' And would remain so for now.

The last person she wanted to talk to was Maddie. She didn't want to hear how wonderful her wedding night had been. Neither did she want to hear a blow-by-blow description of every moment of her honeymoon. Kate had told her sister yesterday not to ring her, but to put her news on social media.

Her mother rolled her eyes in exasperation. 'What's the point of having a mobile if you don't turn it on? Anyway, Maddie sent you a message via me—though I have no idea what she was on about. She said she hopes you did what she told you to last night and that everything worked out. Does that make sense to you?'

'Perfect sense,' Kate replied, and searched her mind for a half-truthful answer which wouldn't shock the pants off her mother. 'Maddie suggested I suck up to Blake Randall and see if I could get myself a part in one of his movies.'

'Goodness. Such language. I'm sure Maddie wouldn't have said it like that. And did you do that? Er…"suck up" to the man?'

'I sure did.'

'And what happened?'

Various images flashed into Kate's head, none of which she could relate to her mother.

'Blake said that since I was a graduate of NIDA he would gladly give me a screen test.'

'Oh, my. What a clever girl your sister is.'

Kate almost lost it then. Truly, did Maddie have to get the credit for *everything*?

Another count to ten.

'So when are you having this screen test?' her mother asked eagerly.

'Blake is organising one for early this evening,' she informed her mother, thinking to herself that she really would have to turn her phone back on in case Byron wanted to ring her. 'He flies back to LA in a couple of days, so time is of the essence. Now, I'm going to go and have a lie-down. Last night has exhausted me. Oh, and don't worry about cooking me dinner tonight, Mum. I won't be coming back here after the audition. Blake's taking me out to dinner.'

'Blake Randall is taking you out to *dinner*?' she said, mouth agape.

'Yes. Do you have a problem with that?'

Her mother tossed her head, the way she did when she couldn't think of what to say for a second or two. 'Well, you're not the sort of girl men like him *usually* take to dinner,' she finally managed. 'There again, I suppose you *did* look surprisingly attractive at the wedding yesterday.'

Her eyes narrowed on Kate's outfit.

'Make sure you wear something better than what you've got on, though. And put on some make-up and do your hair properly. Truly, Kate, it's no wonder you haven't had a boyfriend for years. You simply don't try.'

Kate didn't tell her that Blake had said he liked the way she was dressed today. Her mother probably had no idea he'd driven her home. Blake hadn't come inside. No doubt she thought Kate had taken a taxi home.

'Maybe I don't *want* a boyfriend,' she fired back.

'More likely the one you want you can't have,' her mother muttered.

'Oh, not you too, Mum,' Kate said, hiding her hurt behind irritation. Did *everyone* in her family know about her infatuation with Lachlan?

Yes, of course they did. Time, then, to put things to right.

'If you're talking about Lachlan, then you're

way off the mark. Yes, I did have a crush on him once—but I got over that ages ago. Frankly, I feel sorry for Maddie being married to him. He's not the type to stay faithful.'

'Oh, rubbish! Lachlan adores Maddie. And why would he look elsewhere when he has a wife as beautiful as she is to come home to? They make a brilliant couple. You're just jealous, that's all.'

'No, Mum, I'm not,' she said, with the kind of calmness which came with stating the truth.

Because, as amazing as it seemed, Kate didn't feel jealous of Maddie marrying Lachlan any longer. Not one iota. Her breakdown last night seemed to have somehow banished all the self-destructive emotions which had been affecting both her life and her career for ages. Her depression was gone this morning, along with her lack of spirit. She felt stronger, and a lot more confident.

Kate suspected that her love for Lachlan was on the wane. Her rose-tinted glasses were off where he was concerned and she was finally able to see him for what he was. Not a charming golden boy, but a selfish, arrogant and narcissistic individual, whose only aim in life was his own success. She doubted he loved Maddie any more than Maddie loved him. They were both just trophies for each other. If their marriage lasted two years she'd be surprised.

'Time will tell, I guess,' she added, and walked out of the kitchen.

By the time she reached her bedroom she'd totally dismissed her mother's annoying remarks, plus all thoughts of Lachlan and Maddie. They were not what she wanted to think about right now. She had other things on her mind. Like what *was* she going to wear tonight?

Kate wasn't all that worried about the screen test. She suspected it was just a formality. Blake had said he was going to give her the part anyway; it was only she who had insisted upon a screen test to save her dignity.

She would be wonderful tonight. Her pride demanded it. The same pride that had claimed she would not jump into bed with him just because he'd promised her a job.

His reaction to her making that stand had been very telling. Lord, he'd almost crashed into the car in front of them. Clearly he *had* expected her to sleep with him. But he'd been clever enough to pretend that he hadn't assumed as much.

'Only if you want to…'

What a devious and devilishly tempting invitation *that* was. Because she did want to. Had known it immediately he'd said those words. She hadn't dared look over at him lest he see the heat in her eyes. So she'd looked away until her reaction could be controlled and she could reply with a brilliantly nonchalant remark.

Not that he'd seemed put out by it. No doubt he still thought it was just a matter of time before she gave him what he wanted.

Which was her. In his bed.

The realisation still astounded her. Why *her*? She just didn't understand the ongoing attraction on his part—and certainly not today, when she looked anything but attractive. But she would tonight. Oh, yes, her pride wouldn't let her go for the screen test and then out to dinner with Blake looking, as Maddie would have said, 'like a drack sack'.

She did have some smart outfits—most of them bought for special occasions and nearly all of them chosen for her by Maddie, who admittedly did have good taste and was always on trend with fashion. One particular outfit came to mind. It had been in a shop window, on a tall mannequin with honey-coloured hair rather like hers. Maddie had dragged Kate out clothes shopping back in May, insisting that Kate buy something decent for her engagement party.

'That'd look good on you,' she'd pointed out.

'Maybe...' Kate had replied. 'But it's hardly a ball gown.'

It certainly hadn't been a ball gown, but a knee-length dark red satin cocktail dress, with finger-width straps, snugly fitted, and paired with elegant stiletto shoes. Hanging around the mannequin's neck had been an oval-shaped diamond pendant on a long, fine silver chain.

'No matter. We can look for a ball gown later. We've got all day. Let's go in and try that on you.'

It had suited her, and Maddie had insisted she buy the whole outfit—pendant as well. Thank God it had only been costume jewellery. As it was everything had come to over five hundred dollars. When Kate had dithered about the price Maddie had blithely used her credit card to pay for it all, telling her not to worry, that she wanted her to have it.

'Call it an early birthday present,' she'd said.

Kate had thought the gesture terribly generous of her at the time. Now she wondered if there had been some guilt involved. Whatever—it was a stylish outfit, and one in which she would feel good tonight.

Walking over to her wardrobe, she drew it out and hung it on the door. Then she turned her phone back on—surely Maddie would be in the air by now—lay down on her bed and tried to get some rest.

But her mind wouldn't let her. She kept thinking about Blake lying next to her last night, telling her that she was going to have a very late night tonight. She wondered if he still meant to seduce her, regardless of what he'd said in the car today.

Surely he wouldn't. A *gentleman* wouldn't. A gentleman would keep his word.

But he wasn't *really* a gentleman, was he? It would be naive of her to pretend that he was. Yes, he'd been very kind to her last night. Quite the white knight. But she suspected that gallantry wasn't his true nature; more likely he was a clever and ruthless devil who wasn't beyond using bribery to get a girl into his bed.

He'd used sweet words as well.

I just want to make you happy. To make you smile...

Could she really believe that? Why should he care whether she was unhappy or not? He didn't even know her!

Lachlan had warned her about him—said he was bitter and twisted after what Claudia had done to him, that he used women and treated them badly. But that didn't ring true either. There *was* kindness in him. And compassion. Oh, Lord, she wished she could work him out. He was a conundrum, all right. Still, she really should stick to her guns and not let him seduce her tonight...even if her heart beat faster at the thought.

CHAPTER FOURTEEN

KATE COULDN'T BELIEVE her luck when her mother popped her head around her bedroom door just after four, announcing that she and her father had been invited out for dinner with some friends. They hadn't been guests at the wedding and they wanted to hear all about it.

Off she went, without another word, leaving Kate feeling both grateful and slightly miffed. Which was perverse, she thought as she rose and started getting herself ready. The last thing she wanted was her mother making critical remarks about how she looked. But she might at least have thought to wish her luck with the screen test.

Six o'clock saw her pacing up and down in the front room, watching and waiting for Blake to arrive. By five past six she was beginning to panic. By ten past six she felt sick. He wasn't coming. He'd changed his mind. But if that was so then why hadn't he rung?

It was at this critical point that she remembered he didn't have her phone number. She hadn't given it to him. She didn't have his, either. What if he'd had an accident? What if…?

And then there he was, pulling in to the kerb, jumping out from behind the wheel and striding round the front of the silver Lexus. God, he looked gorgeous, dressed all in black. Black trousers and a black silk shirt, black belt and shoes. Black as his hair. He was frowning, though, his thick dark brows drawn tightly together as he hurried through the wrought-iron gate along the path and up onto the front porch.

Kate resisted flinging open the door before he'd actually rung the bell, but it was a close call. She made him wait a few seconds before she finally turned the knob, doing her best to stay calm and composed and not act like a teenager on her first date.

Actually, it *was* her first date for some years—a fact which should have been depressing. But she had no time for depression tonight. She was having a screen test with the brilliant and wickedly sexy Blake Randall and then going out to dinner with him. How fantastic was *that*?

His deeply set blue eyes gave her one long thorough once-over. 'Good God, Kate, you make it hard on a guy, don't you?' he growled.

'What do you mean?' she asked, pretending not to understand.

'You know exactly what I mean, you bad girl. You could have at least put your hair up into a prissy bun thing instead of leaving it down. I have to tell you now that I have a thing for long hair—especially long, straight, silky honey-coloured hair. I also have a thing for silk dresses and sexy stilettos.'

His sigh was rather melodramatic.

'I thought you wanted me to keep my hands off tonight? Oh, don't bother to answer that,' he swept on, whilst rolling his eyes. 'I'll do my best but I can't promise you anything. Now, let's get going. We're already running late.'

'I have to just get my purse and lock up.'

Kate glanced in the hallway mirror as she hurried past. Her cheeks were flushed and her eyes shining. Lord, he really was a devil. Because she didn't *want* him to keep his hands off, did she?

'So, where's Mommie Dearest?' he asked as they made their way out to the car.

'Visiting some friends.'

'Does she know you're out with me tonight?'

'Oh, yes. I told her. About the screen test *and* the dinner.'

'And?'

'She was surprised at first, and then not very interested.'

'You know, she's just like *my* mother,' he said as he opened the passenger door.

'Oh? In what way?'

'I have an older brother—James. He's the apple of her eye. Can do no wrong. I'm the black sheep in a family of doctors.'

'So you understand, then?' Kate said with a sigh as she climbed in and buckled up.

'I certainly do.'

She closed the door.

'Hold on to this,' he added after getting in behind the wheel and handing her a tablet. 'I've copied the three scenes you're in and brought them up, ready for you to read. You can study them during the drive to Byron's penthouse. That way you'll be prepared by the time we get there. Your character is a secretary who's having an affair with her married boss. She's actually a bit of a closet *femme fatale*—dresses very conservatively in the office and has a witty turn of phrase. I'm sure you'll get the gist once you've read the scenes.'

It hit Kate suddenly that very soon she was actually going to audition for *the* Blake Randall— movie-maker extraordinaire. Up until now it had all seemed somewhat hypothetical. She'd just presumed she would do well. Her confidence was at an all-time high today.

But what if she *didn't* do well? What if she totally stuffed it up?

Nerves gathered in the pit of her stomach as she read through the scenes. The first one wasn't too difficult. Just an office scene with a boss and his PA, with some clever *double entendres* in the dialogue. She thought she could handle the third scene as well. Back in the same office, with the boss breaking off the affair and saying he was going to try to make his marriage work. The PA then told him she'd already got another job and quit, throwing at him the fact that she had bigger fish to fry.

Kate quite liked the idea of playing a bitch. Those sorts of roles were often remembered. But the second scene worried the life out of her.

In a hotel bedroom, it required her character to be in bed, obviously naked under the covers, watching her lover get dressed. She was described as having 'sated, heavy-lidded eyes', with 'a blistering sensuality' in all her movements. In the scene she reached for a cigarette and smoked it slowly, praising her lover's performance and claiming she'd never had better.

'So what do you think?' Blake asked, perhaps sensing her unease.

'I think,' she said slowly, 'that I am going to have difficulty pulling off this role.'

'And why is that?'

Kate knew she had to be honest with him. Or risk making a total fool of herself. But, God, it was going to be hard telling him the truth.

'Well, the thing is…when I act I can usually tap in to some personal experience to help me with the emotions involved. I'm afraid I haven't anything to tap into for this second scene.'

His forehead bunched into a frown. 'What are you saying, Kate? Spell it out for me.'

Kate sighed. 'Well, if you must know, I've never lain in bed watching my lover get dressed. I've never experienced what it is to be sexually sated.

I've only ever had three serious boyfriends, and they *were* just boys, really. And I wasn't ever in a bed—just in the back of a car or on a lumpy sofa. The first time was during my last year in high school. He was a total nerd and hadn't got a clue. Same as me. My other two boyfriends were at university, where I was doing an arts degree and waiting to get into NIDA. They were a bit better than the nerd, but not much.'

'I see,' Blake said thoughtfully. 'So why didn't you have sex with anyone once you went to NIDA? Surely there were some older more experienced chaps there who asked you out?'

'Yes. But I didn't want to go out with them.'

Blake rolled his eyes at her. 'Don't tell me. By then you were madly in love with Lachlan.'

His derisive tone brought an embarrassed heat to Kate's cheeks.

'Oh, Kate, that is just *so* pathetic.'

'I know,' she said in a small voice.

An awkward silence fell, and Kate was startled when she realised they were in the middle of the CBD. Blake suddenly shot across the road and down a ramp which led to an underground car park, braking hard at the bottom so he could activate the security gate. It rose slowly, during which time he threw her a frustrated glance.

'I suppose you haven't dated anyone this year, either?' he ground out.

She shook her head, her mouth having gone dry.

'Truly?' he exclaimed, then muttered very rude words under his breath the whole time it took him to park.

He stomped around to the passenger side of the car, wrenched open the door, snatched up the tablet from her lap and threw it onto the back seat before practically dragging her out of the car and over to the bank of lifts in the corner, glaring at her all the while.

'Not another word,' he snarled when her mouth opened to protest at his caveman-like handling.

Kate backed away from him in the lift, crossing her arms in a huddle of misery when he didn't explain what was going on. Clearly she wasn't going to be doing the screen test. Maybe he was going to give her a lecture about her futile love for Lachlan. He sure as hell was angry with her.

When the lift door opened on the top floor he strode out without looking to see if she was following him or not. She did, of course. What else could she do?

Byron's penthouse was exactly what Kate had expected of a billionaire owner. The rooms were massive and lavishly furnished, and the views from the terrace almost as good as those from the Centrepoint Tower. Everything that proclaimed Sydney one of the most beautiful cities in the world lay before her.

But Kate wasn't in the mood to be impressed. Neither was she interested in being lectured.

'I think,' she said as she stood in the middle of the main living room, her arms crossed once again, but this time with stiff resolve, not misery, 'that you should just take me home. I'd call a taxi, only my purse and my phone are still in your car.'

CHAPTER FIFTEEN

BLAKE WAS TORN between seducing her and slapping her. 'Don't be ridiculous,' he snapped.

'Don't call me ridiculous,' she fired back at him. 'You wanted the truth and I told it to you. I'm sorry if you find it "pathetic" to love someone enough not to want to be with anyone else. No doubt when Claudia dumped you, you went out and shagged everything in sight. But I'm not like that. My feelings run a little deeper.'

'Should I get the violins out now?'

'Oh!' she said, stunned by his insensitive attitude.

Her fingernails dug into her upper arm whilst she struggled with the urge to actually stamp her feet. The only thing stopping her was the fact that he would think her pathetically childish if she did.

'Might I remind you that you would have been quite happy for me to shag you last night?' he threw at her.

Her arms unfolded in a flurry and she strode up close to him, her dark eyes flashing with fury. 'Trust you to bring that up. I was drunk. You *know* I was drunk.'

'Not at first, you weren't. That only came later—after you'd been screwed up by your sweet sister. You wanted me when we were dancing, sweetheart, and don't pretend you didn't. You *still* want me.'

'I do not. I definitely do not. I… I…'

He'd had enough of this—enough of wanting this girl and having to wait until she accepted the fact that she wanted him back. Without hesitation he pulled her into his arms and kissed her, his mouth quite brutal with frustration and a wild, flaring passion.

She froze at first, but then she melted into him, moaning as her arms slid up around his neck, her high, softly rounded breasts pressing hard into his chest. Her gesture of surrender calmed his fury and his mouth gentled on hers, his hands sliding up under her jumper to caress the bare flesh of her lower back. He felt her shiver, then felt himself swell to alarming proportions.

I'm going too fast, came the stern warning. *I*

*have to slow down. Have to. Going too fast isn't
going to work with this girl.*

She might not be a virgin, but she was close to
it.

Kate groaned when his head lifted. She didn't
want him to stop. She'd never been kissed like
that in her life. And it had been mind-blowing.

'So,' he said with a wry smile, 'before I go on
I have a question I must ask you.'

'What?' she asked, her voice sounding dazed.

'Do you want to?'

'Do I want to what?'

He laughed. 'Have you forgotten already the
deal we had? The one where we would only have
sex if you wanted to.'

'Oh. Oh, yes. No. I mean, yes. I did forget about
that.'

'So *do* you want to?'

'Yes,' she said, her heart pounding in her chest.

'You won't accuse me later of taking advantage
of you? Or bribing you into bed with a part in one
of my movies?'

'No.'

'Good. Now, I think this is cause for celebration. I'm sure I saw a bottle of champagne in the fridge earlier. Follow me.'

Kate blinked, then followed him into one of those kitchens that often featured in house and garden magazines. All white and stainless steel, with stone benchtops and no visible drawer handles.

'What are we celebrating?' she asked breathlessly as he retrieved the champagne and found a couple of glasses.

'You discovering that love and great sex don't have to go together.'

The cork popped and he filled the glasses, handing her one before lifting the other to his lips… those cruel-looking lips which only a couple of minutes earlier had rendered her mindless.

'Have you ever had an orgasm?' he asked her, his focus unblinking.

Oh, God, how to answer that?

'Yes,' she admitted, and then swallowed. 'Just not when I'm *with* anyone.'

'Right. Okay. I can work with that. At least you know what a climax feels like.'

Kate could only shake her head at him. 'This is a very intimate conversation.'

'But a very necessary one if I'm to give you what you want. And what you obviously need. Now, let's take our champers along to the master bedroom and get this show on the road.'

'This *show*?' she echoed, appalled and excited at the same time.

'Just an expression, sweetheart. Don't take offence. Sex can be fun, you know. A form of entertainment followed by the most delicious feeling of relaxation. It doesn't have to be all serious with lots of heavy emotion. Being in love can be very disappointing, because when you're in love you try too hard. And trying too hard is the kiss of death where good sex is concerned.'

'I wouldn't know,' she choked out, her stomach suddenly in knots.

'Drink up,' he advised. 'You're looking a little green around the gills.'

'I'm nervous, I guess.' She took a deep swallow, hoping that the alcohol would do the same job as it had last night.

'You weren't nervous when I was kissing you just now. Once we get started again you'll be fine. Trust me.'

She did, letting him lead her down to the most

magnificent bedroom she'd ever seen. He turned to shut the door, leaving her to wander over to the king-sized bed which was dressed all in white, with a fluffy grey throw draped across the foot of the bed.

She took another swallow of champagne as she stared at the bed and tried to imagine being naked in it with Blake by her side.

'Here, give me that,' Blake said, taking the glass from her trembling hand and putting it down with his on one of the bedside tables. 'You're thinking too much,' he said, and drew her into his arms, his eyes darkening as they roved over her probably anxious-looking face.

Just kiss me, she thought breathlessly. *Kiss me and take me again to that place where the real world recedes and there's nothing but your mouth on mine and your hands all over me.*

He kissed her, but slowly this time, tenderly, his lips roving over hers until they gasped apart. She sucked in sharply when his tongue-tip met hers, moaning for more. But he didn't ravage her mouth as she'd thought she wanted him too. Instead he made love to it, giving her pleasure and frustration in equal parts. His hands were gentle as well—not delving boldly under her top as they had before, but running up and down her spine on top of her clothes.

When he stopped, she groaned in protest.

His head lifted and he smiled down at her. 'Softly, softly, catchee monkey,' he murmured.

'What?'

'Nothing. Come on. Sit down.'

'Sit down?'

'Yes. I want to get rid of those heels for starters.'

She sank down on the side of the bed, stunned when Blake knelt at her feet and slowly removed her left shoe.

Once it was disposed of he glanced up at her, his smile wry. 'I'm always removing your footwear.' Then he bent his head and slipped off her right stiletto, easing it off and tossing it aside.

'Now,' he went on as he stood up, 'as gorgeous as your top is, I want that gone as well.'

Kate immediately thought of her simple white cotton bra—which, whilst not old, wasn't very new either. Or very sexy.

Before she could worry too much about it he'd removed her pendant, dropping it on the bedside table before slipping the thin straps of her dress over her shoulders.

'If I'd known I was going to d-do this,' she stammered, 'I would have worn some s-sexier underclothes. Not that I have any…' she muttered under her breath.

'Come now, Kate,' Blake said with laughing eyes. 'What about that black number you had on last night? That had me salivating, it was so sexy.'

'Maddie bought that for me.'

'Oh, yes—Maddie the sex kitten. Or at least she thinks she is.'

'You don't think so?'

'I already told you, Kate. She's not my type. Now, *you*…' he continued as he reached around and unhooked her bra. 'You are definitely my type.'

Kate's heartbeat stopped when he peeled off her bra and left her sitting there naked to the waist. Yet, oddly, she felt more excited than embarrassed. And totally breathless. After a few dizzying seconds she began breathing again, hard and fast, her chest expanding as she sucked in much-needed air.

Blake's eyes dropped to her breasts with their

fiercely erect nipples, all tight and hard and eager for his hands, or his mouth.

'Oh, yes,' he said thickly. '*Definitely* my type.'

Just when she thought he was going to do what she craved he knelt down again, reaching up under the skirt of her dress and pulling down her white cotton panties. And then he was pushing her back onto the bed and lifting her dress, putting his mouth not to her aching nipples but to that part of her which she hadn't realised until that moment was far needier.

She gasped, then groaned. His fingers and tongue were doing things to her that had never been done before. They made her burn for him, made her incapable of stopping him. She was mindless. Tortured. Rapturous. All she knew was that she couldn't bear it if he stopped. She was so close to coming. *So* close.

He stopped.

'No, don't stop!' she cried out.

'Have to, sweetness,' he said, standing up and pulling her skirt down again.

'But I was about to…you know—' She broke off and sat up, feeling flustered and frustrated.

'Yes, I know. But so was I.'

'Oh,' she said, only then noting his ragged breathing.

'Never happened to me before,' he ground out, and stared at her as if it was *her* fault.

'I'm sorry,' she said, which was crazy. What was she saying sorry for?

'I suppose it has been several weeks since I've had sex,' he muttered, as if he was looking for a valid reason for his lack of control.

'Really?' That surprised Kate. She'd always thought powerful, good-looking men like Blake never did without sex for long. She'd imagined they always had women throwing themselves at them.

'Really and truly.' He sighed a heavy sigh, at the same time running his hands agitatedly through his hair. 'Under the circumstances, best we move on to the real thing.'

CHAPTER SIXTEEN

'I JUST NEED to go to the bathroom first,' Blake lied. 'Meanwhile, why don't you get into bed?' He made his escape, desperate for a minute or two by himself.

Blake closed the door firmly behind him, still rattled by what had just happened. He simply couldn't believe he'd almost lost it, having always prided himself on his sexual skills—especially his ability to control his body and not act like some horny teenager whose only aim was getting his rocks off.

It was especially embarrassing given Kate's sexual history. He'd been determined to give her the time of her life, and what had he done? Almost blown it—that was what he'd done.

Maybe he'd been trying too hard to please her.

That last thought bothered him. He wasn't usually a try-hard.

He glanced at himself in the bathroom mirror,

shocked by what he saw. Not his usual cavalier self, but someone who was beginning to care too much. About her. That was the problem. It had been the problem from the first moment he'd seen her, walking down that staircase, looking haunted and terrified.

It annoyed the hell out of him that she was in love with Lachlan—that she probably fantasised about him when she made herself come in her lonely bed at night. He wanted to obliterate that bastard from her mind...wanted to give her something or someone better to dream about.

And that would be you, would it, Blake Randall? You—a man who doesn't even believe in love, or romance, or any of the things that seem to matter to women? What can you give Kate that would really matter to her? That would be a positive influence in her life? That would make her happy? Or at least happier.

The chance for a successful acting career, he supposed. And a healthier attitude to sex. Sex didn't *have* to be connected to love. Much better to be just about physical pleasure. And fun. That was what he had told her, and that was what he was going to deliver.

So he cared about her as well? So what? He was allowed to care, wasn't he? There was no crime in that.

'Right,' he told himself sternly, and turned to flush the toilet before heading for the bathroom door.

Kate stiffened when she heard the toilet flush. She had taken off her dress and dived naked into the bed, shivering a little at the coolness of the sheets. Not that the room was cold, the penthouse obviously had ducted air-conditioning and heating.

Her heart jumped when he emerged, but his ready smile calmed her a little.

'Sorry about that,' he said, and whipped his shirt up off over his head.

Kate hadn't really thought about what his body might look like without clothes. She'd known he was tall and slim, with nice shoulders and olive skin. But the reality was better than she could have imagined, with his well-toned arms and chest, and a smattering of dark, sexy curls arrowing down to his navel.

'You must work out a lot,' she said, just for something to say. Better than sitting there ogling him.

He shrugged as he took his wallet out of his pocket and placed it by the bed. 'I have a gym in my home. Everyone works out in Hollywood. Everyone except the really fat-cat producers. All they have to do is go to lunch and show their credit cards.'

'I jog sometimes,' she said, trying not to stare. But it was getting harder now he'd taken off his trousers. 'And I walk a lot. I don't have a car.'

'You have a great figure,' he complimented her, sitting down on the side of the bed in his black underpants and taking off his shoes and socks. 'I adore it. I like natural.'

'Well, I'm certainly that.'

Maddie had had a boob job when she was twenty, which her parents had happily paid for. But Kate didn't mind her B-cup breasts, believing they went with her more athletic shape. Her agent had once criticised her smallish bust, but she'd ignored him. Thank goodness she had. She rather suspected Blake wouldn't have fancied her if her breasts had been surgically enhanced.

Relief swamped Kate when Blake kept his back to her as he took off his underpants. Hopefully he would just dive into bed the way she had and she wouldn't have to look at his penis.

But he didn't oblige, turning to pick up his wallet and extract a condom first. He was fully erect. Impressively so. Her mouth went dry at the thought of what was to come. Her heartbeat quickened.

She looked away while he drew the condom on, not turning back to face him until she felt the mattress dip.

'Don't go shy on me,' he told her as he put his arms around her and drew her close.

She looked up into his eyes. 'I'm not shy so much as nervous. I need you to kiss me again.'

'And *I* need to kiss you again,' he replied, and did so.

It was even better with their naked bodies pressed against each other. So exciting and intimate, making her quickly hungry for more. Not just more kissing. More bodily contact. She wanted him inside her. No, *needed* him inside her. Her leg lifted to curve over his hip, giving him access to her body, urging him without words to take her. Now. *Now!*

He did her silent bidding, his body surging into

hers, rolling her onto her back and going even deeper. His mouth moved away from hers, his eyes hot and hungry as he began to move. She moved with him, lifting her legs high onto his back, clinging to him and almost sobbing with pleasure. Her heart was squeezed tight in her chest, her flesh gripping his like a vice.

She was just beginning to think she might have a heart attack when she came with a rush, her release so brilliant and violent that she screamed out. 'Blake! Oh, Blake!'

His climax quickly followed hers, and his own cry of release was loud and primal, his whole body shuddering as he came. Finally he collapsed across her and buried his face in her hair.

Kate revelled in the feel of his weight, holding him tight lest he try to withdraw. She didn't feel all limp and sleepy, like she'd read in books. She felt more awake and alive than she'd ever felt before. She could hardly wait to do it again. And again. She wanted to try everything with him— every possible position—and not just in this bed.

Her fantasies were endless and wild. She was envisaging herself doing the sort of things Maddie did with Lachlan.

Lachlan...

It came as a shock to Kate that she could think of Lachlan whilst in bed with another man and not feel a single bit of regret that it wasn't him in bed with her. If anything, the thought of him vaguely repulsed her. How odd. Was she over him at last? She rather suspected she was. Whatever—she'd certainly reached a point where her feelings for her brother-in-law were not going to stop her from enjoying life. From enjoying Blake.

Kate stirred beneath him. Blake lifted his head and smiled down at her. She smiled back at him—a slow, sensual smile which echoed her satisfaction and hinted at her ongoing desires.

'Methinks,' he said, with a sexy glitter in his eyes, 'that you won't have too much trouble with that movie role after all.'

CHAPTER SEVENTEEN

'YOU'RE DOING *WHAT*?'

Kate ignored her mother's horrified reaction—at least on the surface. She'd known what to expect and had steeled herself accordingly.

'You heard what I said, Mum,' she replied coolly. 'I'm going to Hollywood. My screen test went very well last night. Blake said the part is definitely mine.'

Lord, she really *was* a good actress. Not a hint of irony on her face. Nor shame. Not that she intended to feel shame over what she'd done with Blake last night. Or what she intended to do in the future. He'd opened a whole new world to her—one she wanted to explore and enjoy to the full. And she wasn't just thinking about her career.

'He's also kindly offered to let me stay at his place until I get on my feet.'

She couldn't wait to live in the same house as

him, to be with him every night. Even if it only lasted a short while.

Janice Holiday's eyes narrowed on her daughter. 'Now, why would he do something like that?'

'Why not? He's a kind and generous man. Look at the way he stepped in and organised that lovely and totally free venue for Maddie's wedding, saving Maddie from a nervous breakdown and saving you and Dad an absolute fortune. He didn't have to do that.'

'We *did* pay for the marquee,' Janice huffed. *'And* the catering. Besides, it was Lachlan he was helping out—not us. *He's* the one who's making Blake Randall a small fortune.'

'I think the shoe is on the other foot, Mum. It's Blake who's making *Lachlan* a small fortune. Without him Lachlan would still be a struggling actor, trying to make ends meet.'

'Oh, rubbish! Anyone with any brains can see it's Lachlan's talent which has put Blake Randall on the map. Without him that man would be an also-ran, making boring little movies which no one would go to see.'

Kate had no intention of arguing with her mother.

Experience had taught her it was a total waste of time. She always had to have the last word.

'Don't think I don't know what's going on,' her mother continued, her tone caustic. 'Men like that always want something in return for their so-called generosity. You slept with him last night, didn't you?'

Kate drew herself up to her full five foot nine inches, setting reproachful eyes on her mother. 'I did not,' she denied, quite truthfully.

They hadn't slept one bit—either before or after dinner.

'Well, it's just a matter of time. When are you seeing him next? Today, I'll bet.'

'No, I'm not.' *Worse luck.* 'He's playing golf with Byron today, and has an important business dinner tonight. Then he's booked to fly back to LA early tomorrow morning. I plan to follow as soon as I can. I checked the visa situation online and Australians can get their visa waivered—but you have to wait three days after applying. I'm allowed to stay for ninety days before reapplying.'

Her mother looked doubtful. 'Surely that would only cover tourists? Not people who are going to work in the country?'

'No, it says you can be going there for business or pleasure. And Blake said once I'm there and have a contract in my hand I can apply for some other visa which I will eventually need.'

'So you haven't signed a contract yet?'

'No. Not yet. But I will once I get over there.'

'And who's going to pay for your plane ticket to get you over there? *You* don't have that sort of money. Or is our generous Mr Randall going to pay for that as well?'

Blake had offered to do just that, but Kate had refused. She didn't mind temporarily staying in his house as a guest, but she wasn't going to let him pay for other things. That would make her feel like a kept woman. All she wanted from Blake was a helping hand with her career. Oh, yes, and lots of lovely sex.

'I was hoping that you and Dad would buy me a return ticket. After all, I've never asked you to buy me anything before.'

'We give you free board and lodging. I would have thought that was enough.'

'You gave Maddie free board and lodging too,' Kate pointed out, keeping her temper with difficulty. 'Yet she was earning good money as a receptionist. On top of which you bought her a car *and* paid for her to have a boob job. Not to mention a thousand other expensive items over the years. I have never asked you for *anything*, Mum,' she said, her voice rising a few decibels. *'Never.'*

Her father suddenly appeared in the doorway, surprising Kate. She'd thought he'd be at work by now. Possibly he had a flex day. He sometimes took one on a Monday, and he was still in his dressing gown.

'What are you two arguing about?' he asked wearily.

'Kate wants us to buy her a plane ticket to go to Hollywood. A return ticket, no less. She's had this ridiculous offer of a movie role from Blake Randall and she thinks he's doing it out of the goodness of his heart. She doesn't realise there's no such thing as a free lunch. He'll want his pound of flesh in return. And it's not as though she has a contract in her hand. On top of that, she's going to stay at his house. Well, I *ask* you. It's as plain as the nose on your face what he wants. Though Lord knows why. I mean, it's not as though Kate is a raving beauty, like our Maddie. I could understand it if Blake Randall wanted *her* for a part in one of his movies. What do you think, Neville?'

'What do I *think*, Janice?'

He answered in a tone that Kate had never heard before. It was rather cold and very firm—not what she'd expected from her hen-pecked father.

'I think we should not only support our daughter and buy her a return ticket to LA, but that we should make it business class. It's a long trip, and I wouldn't want her getting there looking all tired and drawn. Unlike you, I have every respect for Blake Randall, and I don't think he has some dastardly ulterior motive in offering Kate a part in one of his movies. Why should he when she's such a brilliant actress? Have you forgotten how wonderful she was in those plays they put on at NIDA? *She* was the star—not Lachlan. I dare say Blake Randall was already aware of her talent, even before her screen test.

'And by the way,' he added, whilst his wife's mouth was still hanging open. 'Kate might not be what *some* people call a raving beauty, but she is very attractive, with classic features which will last long after most women's faces fall apart. Now, I am going back to bed. I'm not at my best this morning. Please give Kate our credit card, Janice. And Kate? Well done. You're a hard worker and a fine actress and you deserve all the success in the world.'

'I have to confess, Blake,' Kate told him when he rang her later, as promised, 'that I didn't know whether to laugh or cry. I mean, it was amusing to see my mother stuck for words for once, but... but...' She felt suddenly choked up and couldn't go on.

'But you were touched by your father's magnificent defence of you?'

'Yes. Yes, I was.'

The things he'd said about her had meant so much. Kate hadn't realised how hurt she'd been all these years by his seeming to favour Maddie. Now she saw that it had been more her mother doing the favouring than him. He'd just gone along with what his wife and Maddie wanted to keep the peace. Of course Maddie *was* very charming— and very manipulative. It was awfully hard to say no to her. Kate also conceded that she herself had been silly to stay in the background all the time...

not asking for anything, and playing the victim, in a way.

No more of that, she decided. She was done with playing second fiddle to her sister.

'How was your golf game with Byron?' she asked, lying down on her bed and stretching out. 'Did you win?'

'Did I win, she asks? Of course I won. In the end. I let him get close to me in the first nine, but I slaughtered him in the second.'

Kate smiled. He really was terribly arrogant. But she still liked him.

'Poor Byron...'

Blake laughed. 'Hardly poor. He just keeps on getting richer. That man has the Midas touch when it comes to investments. I'm always happy when he comes aboard as co-producer on one of my movies. They never bomb. Not that I *ever* make duds, of course. Anyway, I told him about the movie you're going to be in and he's agreed to put a good chunk of money in it. In the past he's only ever wanted to invest in Lachlan's movies, but he's willing to take a chance now on anything I recommend.'

'Maybe he thinks *you've* got the Midas touch?'

'There's nothing magical about *my* success. It took me years of trial and error to work out what worked in movies and what didn't. Even so, you can never be one hundred percent sure of a positive reception. Film audiences can be very fickle.'

'Speaking of movies,' Kate said, 'I've been thinking about my part and I have a suggestion to make. I hope you don't mind.'

'Good grief! Her first movie role and she's already trying to change the script,' he said, but he was laughing.

'Not at all. I just don't like the part where I reach for a cigarette. I mean, I *hate* smoking, and so do most people now. I know I'm supposed to be a bad girl in this movie, but her smoking doesn't really add anything to the role and I'd rather not do it. Couldn't I reach for a glass of champagne instead? That would be just as effective.'

'I don't see why not. Is that all?'

'Oh, yes. Absolutely.'

'Good. I'm not a man who likes it when actors try to change my scripts.'

'I wouldn't dare.'

He laughed. 'I think perhaps you would. In time.

God, I wish I didn't have to go to this dinner tonight. I'd much rather be in bed with you.'

'*I'd* rather you were in bed with me too.'

'Have you booked your flight yet?'

'Yes. I fly out late Friday evening and I get into LAX around six Friday evening your time. Australia is seventeen hours ahead of you, so I found out.'

'It's a non-stop flight, then?'

'Yes.' She gave him the flight number.

'I'll just write that down,' he said. 'You'll be glad you're flying business class.'

'I still can't believe Mum and Dad forked out that much money. Maddie's going to be so jealous.'

'How will she know? She's in Europe on her honeymoon for the next month or so.'

'That won't stop her ringing Mum every day.'

'I will never understand this obsession women have for talking on the phone all the time. I can't stand it.'

'You're talking to *me* on the phone right now.'

'You're the exception to my rule. I like talking to you. Of course I'd prefer to be talking to you with your naked body next to me, but since I can't have that, then I have to settle for this. Damn—it's just occurred to me that I won't be enjoying that privilege again for over four days. You wouldn't consider catching a taxi here at around eleven tonight, would you? I should be finished with my business dinner by then. You could stay the night, perhaps?'

It was tempting. *Very.*

'I'm sorry, Blake, but I can't do that. I told my mother I didn't sleep with you last night and I couldn't stand the next few days if she found out I'd lied. Which she would if I did what you're asking.'

'Fair enough. It'll probably be better for the waiting. Anticipation is one of the best forms of foreplay.'

She could believe that. She was already turned on, just thinking about being with him again.

'Your silence betrays you, sweet Kate. Just think what we could have got up to tonight. There are so many things I want to do to you and haven't done yet. We could have had such fun.'

Kate was glad he couldn't see her red cheeks. Or hear her thudding heart. But something—a kind of pride, perhaps—demanded that she did not let him think he could do whatever he liked to her and she wouldn't object.

Last night had been amazing, sexually, showing her how good it was to move on with her life, to put Lachlan behind her and find pleasure in another man's body. But that didn't mean she was going to become Blake's mindless plaything. She did have a mind of her own and she aimed to use it.

'There are things I want to do to *you* too, Blake,' she countered coolly. 'But, as you just said, it will be all be better for the waiting.'

Now *he* was the one who was silent. But then he laughed—a low, sexily sardonic laugh.

'I'll meet you at the airport,' he said, letting the matter drop.

Kate's independent mode was not easily dropped. 'Won't that be a bother? You'll have to pay for parking, and maybe wait if the flight is late, or customs are slow. I could just as easily catch a taxi if you give me the address.'

'*Cab*, Kate. In LA they're called cabs.'

'Oh. A cab, then.'

'No, I'll meet you,' he insisted. 'Carlos can drive

me and wait somewhere until we're ready to be picked up.'

'You have a chauffeur?'

She shouldn't be surprised, but she was, which showed her that she hadn't truly absorbed just yet how wealthy Blake was. The penthouse she'd spent last night in hadn't been his, after all.

'Not exactly,' Blake replied. 'Though I often use Carlos to drive me places. Carlos is my house-keeper's husband. Her name's Juanita. She does the cooking and cleaning. Carlos is handyman, gardener and sometimes chauffeur. They're from Mexico, though they've lived in the USA for over twenty years. They came with the house and I thank God every day for them both. They're a great couple. Good workers and always cheerful. I feel very blessed to have them.'

Kate was taken aback by this last statement.

'I didn't know you were religious,' she said.

'What? Oh, the "blessed" thing. No, I'm not—but most of America is. I dare say I've picked up a few phrases.'

'I rather like it. It's sweet.'

'Americans *can* be sweet. But sometimes their sweetness is only on the surface—especially in

Hollywood, and especially in the movie business. Thankfully Carlos and Juanita didn't come to LA to try their hand at acting. All they wanted, they told me, was a better life for themselves and their children.'

'They have children?'

'Unfortunately, no. They weren't lucky that way. Juanita said they left it too late before they tried and then it didn't happen. But they're not bitter about it. They're thankful for what they have.'

'They sound like a great couple.'

'Yes, you'll like them.'

'I'm sure I will. And I'm sure I'll like Holly-wood—no matter what dire warnings you give me. I can't wait to get there.'

'And I can't wait for you to get there too,' he said, with heavy irony in his voice.

Kate laughed. 'Will you stop that? Let's talk about something else besides sex.'

But even as she said the word it occurred to Kate that a man like Blake would rarely have to wait for the pleasure of a woman in his bed. Maybe he *wouldn't* wait. Maybe when he got back to LA he'd ring up one of his lady-friends—he was sure to have heaps—and have her fill the gap in his sex life until Kate arrived on the scene.

Jealousy jabbed at Kate. Yet it wasn't the same kind of jealousy she'd used to feel about Lachlan and Maddie. Strangely, this was more disturbing—and infinitely more confusing. Because she didn't love Blake the way she'd loved Lachlan. She didn't love Blake *at all*! She liked him a lot— found him terribly sexy and quite fascinating. But she didn't want to marry him or spend the rest of her life with him. She didn't romanticise her feelings for him in any way. She saw them for what they were.

Why the jealousy, then?

Kate decided it was just her newly found feminine ego—the ego that thought her performance in bed last night had been oh, *so* good.

Silly Kate. Don't go thinking you're anything special to Blake, because you aren't. Your mother is right. There's no such thing as a free lunch. Yes, Blake might want to help you with your career—he probably gets off on the idea of being a magnanimous mentor—but there is a price to be paid. In his bed.

Just because you'll love every minute of it, that

doesn't mean sleeping with Blake is without danger. What if you do fall in love with the man? It could happen now that Lachlan seems to be history.

Never forget that Blake doesn't want a real relationship with you, came the stern warning. *There is no future with him—no prospect of you becoming a proper girlfriend. And if you can't come to terms with that before you go to LA then you're a fool and you shouldn't go.*

Kate resolved not to be a fool. Because nothing was going to stop her going to Hollywood.

'What would you like to talk about?' Blake asked.

'Movies. What else?'

CHAPTER EIGHTEEN

BLAKE STOOD IN the arrivals area, close to the gate where Kate was due to emerge. Her flight had landed a good twenty minutes ago, but still there was no sign of her. Patience was not his strong suit, and his agitation was increasing with each passing second.

And then suddenly there she was, pulling a black suitcase behind her, her eyes scanning the crowd for him. She didn't see him straight away, giving Blake a thankful few seconds to drink her in unobserved.

She was a sight for sore eyes, despite being dressed in sensible travelling clothes—stone-washed grey jeans, a white T-shirt and a black jacket. Hardly an outfit which would usually fire up his male hormones. But it did. As did everything else about her. Her hair was bundled up on top of her head in a haphazard style which he found extremely sexy, and her face was freshly made-up, bringing attention to her lovely dark eyes and wide, luscious mouth.

Blake could not wait to get her home and alone. He'd had enough of just talking to her over the past few days, having spent more time on the phone to Kate than he had with any woman in his life—including his ex.

Aside from their long discussions about movies and acting, he now knew more about Kate than he'd ever found out about Claudia. She'd told him all about her upbringing—including her not very happy days at school, when she'd been totally overshadowed by her younger's sister vibrant personality, her self-esteem plummeting until she'd discovered acting in the school's drama class. Once portraying another character, her confidence had soared. Though it had always shrunk again once she was off the stage.

There had been no boyfriends for her—not until she'd met Tom, the boy who made the sets for the drama class, who had basically been as introverted as she was. Blake already knew that sex with Tom had been ordinary, at best. But at least she'd had a boyfriend for a while.

Her meagre sexual experiences at university had

been of a similar ilk. Then, of course, had come the fiasco with Lachlan. It pleased Blake that Kate could talk about Lachlan now with more pragmatism. Her rose-tinted glasses were well and truly off. Who knew? Maybe she was finally getting over the guy? He sure hoped so. She deserved better than a self-obsessed narcissist who would never love anyone as much as he loved himself.

Suddenly she spied him, her face lighting up, her expression a mixture of joy and relief.

He moved forward, all smiles, taking the case away from her. 'You made it,' he said, and bent to peck her on the cheek. Blake was not a big hugger and kisser in public.

'Only just. My shoulder bag sparked off some machine and I was taken aside like I was a criminal. They emptied out all the contents and checked it over for drugs. It came back clear, of course. I mean, I would *never* do drugs. Still, I almost wet myself with terror whilst I was waiting.'

Blake nodded in sympathy. 'That happened to me once. Puts the wind up you, doesn't it? Still, store that emotion for when you have to act a part that requires terror. Nothing is wasted when you're an actor. Or a scriptwriter, for that matter.'

Kate took the bag off her shoulder and sighed as she stared into it. 'They just threw everything back in. My make-up is all over the place. And they've squashed up the magazine I bought.'

She pulled it out. Blake recognised the beaming couple on the cover immediately. He would hardly forget *that* bride and groom in a hurry. Clearly Maddie hadn't either, no matter how pragmatic their conversation over the phone. The headline caught his eye too: *Hunky Aussie Actor Weds*.

'I couldn't resist,' she said a little sheepishly. 'I saw it on a stand at the airport in Sydney and just had to buy it.'

An emotion Blake wasn't overly familiar with grabbed at his insides. It took him a split second to recognise it as jealousy.

Blake had experienced jealousy when Claudia had dumped him for that Hollywood fat-cat— along with fury and confusion and a whole raft of other conscience-blasting emotions.

He hadn't been able to think straight, but his arrogant male ego had refused to let him cry, or get counselling for his hurt. Instead he'd behaved badly, working his pain out by indulging in revenge sex with a couple of actresses who had made a play for him.

Thankfully, neither of them had been the type to suffer from a broken heart afterwards, but one of them had told him in no uncertain terms what she thought of his callous attitude the morning after. It had been a sobering experience, and one which he'd taken to heart. After that he'd been more careful with women, always making it clear that dating him wasn't a long-term proposition. He was into flings and affairs, not relationships.

He had had what might be termed a girlfriend or two since his divorce, but nothing serious. He certainly had never invited a girl to stay at his place for more than a night.

Or he hadn't until Kate had come along.

It worried him now…what he was getting himself into with this girl. If he didn't know better he might think he was falling in love. Which would never do. If and when he was foolish enough to fall in love it wouldn't be with someone who'd spent the last four years of her life dreaming of another man. For all he knew Kate was still dreaming of him. She might talk big about moving on, but she'd bought that magazine, hadn't she? Had probably spent hours during the flight admiring photos of him and wishing she were in Maddie's place.

'Not that I really wanted the damned thing,' Kate went on. 'I was just curious. I also hoped there would be some pictures of you and me—but, no, they were all of Lachlan and Maddie. Typical.'

And without a backward glance, she tossed the magazine into a nearby bin, before throwing him a remorseful glance.

'You didn't want to look at it, did you?'

Blake could have kissed her. She wasn't pining for that fool, and the thought brought him a type of joy which might have worried him if he hadn't been so relieved.

'I've already seen the photos, Kate. As soon as that magazine came out they were all over social media.'

'Oh, yes. I imagine they are. I'm not into social media. But Maddie is.'

'And Lachlan as well. He's an incorrigible show pony. Can't say I'm overly keen on the way technology has gone. But it's the way of the world, Kate. Speaking of technology,' he went on ruefully, and whipped out his phone, 'I'll just text

Carlos and tell him to make his way to the pick-up point.'

'And I'll text Mum and Dad—let them know I've arrived safely.'

They both finished together, and Kate turned her phone off before dropping it back into her bag. Blake slipped his phone into his pocket, then took her elbow.

'Let's go.' Blake pulled her suitcase along behind them. 'I have a web page, of course,' he continued as they walked companionably together. 'And various other links which my PA attends to. But that's for business only. I like to keep my personal life to myself.'

'I do too. I don't understand why ordinary people—not celebrities—take photos of everything they do, even the most mundane things, then post it somewhere on the internet for people to see. I just don't get it.'

'I suppose it's a form of entertainment. And it makes them feel important. Like they're celebrities.'

'But it opens them up to criticism and bullying.'

'True. But that's become a fact of modern life, too. Social media isn't going to go away, so you might as well embrace it. You have to develop a thick skin, Kate, if you want to be a success in Hollywood. Because if and when that happens you'll be criticised to death over everything from your clothes to your weight and whoever you have by your side. You'll be stalked by the paparazzi and your life generally won't be yours.'

Kate stopped and stared at him. 'You make success sound so attractive!'

Blake shrugged. 'It's a sink-or-swim existence, being in the spotlight, but it can be very exciting. Though only if you don't let it go to your head... like someone who will remain nameless.'

'Oh, I suppose you mean Lachlan.'

'Lachlan who?' he said, with just a touch of malice. 'Ah, here's our ride.'

CHAPTER NINETEEN

KATE GAPED WHEN a white limousine braked abruptly at the kerb, next to where they were standing.

'Oh, my goodness!' she exclaimed, both impressed and slightly overawed.

Blake grinned at her. 'When in Rome, you know...'

The driver—a short, middle-aged man with black curly hair and swarthy skin—jumped out from behind the wheel, flashing Kate a welcoming smile before grabbing her suitcase.

'Better get inside, boss,' Carlos said, with only the slightest accent. 'The Indians are circling.'

'What does he mean?' Kate said as Blake yanked open the back door.

Just then a photographer stepped forward from Lord knew where and snapped a couple of shots of them both. Blake didn't say a word, just hustled Kate into the limo, throwing the photographer a big smile before climbing in after her and shutting the door. By this time Carlos was back behind the wheel and they were soon off.

'Carlos, this is Kate,' Blake introduced. 'Kate, this is Carlos.'

'Hello, Carlos.'

'Welcome to LA, Kate. Sorry I was a bit slow picking you up, boss. Friday evenings, you know… Lots of comings and goings.'

'No sweat, Carlos. If I didn't want to be photographed then I shouldn't have had you drive up in a limo.'

Carlos laughed.

'You didn't mind us being photographed?' Kate asked Blake.

'Hell, no. It's good publicity for me—and for you. Those photos will be all over the internet somewhere within the hour—with a caption something like *Blake Randall meets mystery woman at airport. A new star or a new girlfriend?*'

'Goodness!' Kate exclaimed, not sure if she was thrilled or anxious.

She didn't like the thought of her family seeing it—especially her mother. But even if she didn't see it, Maddie would. And she rang her mother every day. Being on her honeymoon wouldn't stop her. She could just imagine their conversation. Maddie might have urged Kate to make a play for Blake, but she wouldn't have dreamt that her sister would end up in LA, staying at his house.

Actually, Kate was finding it all a bit surreal herself. She could hardly believe that she was here. The last few days had seemed endless. Blake had rung her every day, which had been wonderful, but it had made her crave to be with him again. She'd almost forgotten her career for a while, her focus more on the sexual side of things. Yet they were both entwined, weren't they?

'Don't let it bother you,' Blake said, perhaps sensing her sudden unease. 'The Hollywood publicity mill runs on endless speculation. Best not to fight it or it only gets worse. Go with the flow. Have fun with it.'

'Fun?' she echoed.

He grinned over at her, then picked up her hand and kissed it like a gallant gentleman of old. *'Oui, mademoiselle,'* he said, sounding like Maurice Chevalier in *Gigi*.

Their eyes met over her hand and the air around them thickened with instant desire. How handsome he was—and very sophisticated-looking, dressed in a charcoal-grey business suit, white shirt and silver tie. Her heart had fluttered when she'd first sighted him at the airport. It had also pushed firmly aside any qualms she'd had over this trip. For she'd seen real affection in his eyes. Real caring.

Now all she saw was hunger—a raw, animal hunger which threatened to transcend her own.

A highly erotic shudder rippled down her spine and he saw it, his eyes darkening. He enfolded her hands in both of his and pulled her hard against his side. She dropped her head to his shoulder with a sigh. This would have to do. *For now.*

'If photographers are going to pop out from behind every pole or door,' she said, after a couple of minutes wallowing in the warmth of his body, 'I'll have to watch how I look when I go out.'

'You always look gorgeous,' he told her.

She smiled up at him. 'I really don't. But it's sweet of you to say so.'

'Did you bring some going out clothes with you?'

'Sort of…'

'What does that mean?'

'I suspect that my version of "going out" clothes falls a little short of the Hollywood version.'

'Maybe. Maybe not. People don't always get dressed up to the nines here. It can be a very casual city. But if you like I'll take you clothes-shopping tomorrow.'

'Will you?' she said, smiling wryly to herself as she recalled a scene from one of her favourite movies. 'In Rodeo Drive?'

'Of course.'

Her eyes slanted up to his. 'Thank you, but I think I should make do with what I have until I earn some money,' she said, knowing that that would be taking things a step too far. As it was, the balance of their relationship was a bit iffy. No way was she going to let him start buying her clothes. 'Actually, my wardrobe is not too bad at the moment. Dad forked out some more money for me—behind Mum's back, of course—and I went shopping this week. Also, fortunately the weather here is similar to that in Sydney at the moment.'

'So it is. Your spring is much the same as our fall.'

'Fall? Oh, you mean autumn.'

'Yes.'

'You seem to have become very American in the short time you've been over here.'

'Actually, I *am* half-American.'

Kate sat up straight and stared at him, the action pulling her hand out of his grasp. 'How did that come about?'

'My mother's American. My dad met her when they were both studying medicine at Harvard. I was born over here—in Boston. They moved to Sydney just after I turned one. I have dual citizenship.'

'You still sound like an Aussie to me,' Carlos piped up. 'More so than Kate.'

'For which I am grateful,' Blake said.

Kate settled back in the seat and put her head on his shoulder again. 'The teachers at NIDA insisted that we get rid of any strong Australian accent. They said it was a negative when it came to getting work.'

'That's absolutely correct. Especially in Hollywood. They like an international-sounding voice. Not too many roles over here for Australians. By the way—did you bring all your references from NIDA?'

'What? Oh, yes—yes, of course.'

'Good. We'll need those to help get you the necessary visa for you to work here.'

Kate frowned. 'There won't be a problem with that, will there?'

'I doubt it. I've hired the best lawyer in LA to process your application. Now, no more work talk. We're almost home.'

'Already?' Kate's head swivelled to see where she was.

'West Hollywood isn't that far from the airport,' Blake explained.

The limousine wound its way up a rather steep road, with houses set back behind high security walls and often behind tall trees. Not that she could see them very well. Night had fallen, and whilst there were street lights they were few and far between. Up and up the road went, and one side of the road was now higher than the other.

Kate was craning her neck to peer up at the spectacular properties on the high side when Carlos pulled into a wide driveway in front of some tall wooden gates fixed into an equally tall stone wall. She couldn't see through that either, but she could see over it.

Up high, on a hill beyond, sat a house which

took Kate's breath away. Whilst possibly not the biggest house in the world, its contemporary architecture could not help but impress. Over the wall she could see two rectangular-shaped floors, white in colour and cement rendered, the top one smaller than the one below. Both had wide covered decks which were lit up and no doubt provided splendid views of the surroundings.

Kate suspected, however, even before the gates opened, that there would be another floor out of sight. And she was right.

The bottom floor was even larger, encompassing a six-car garage, a fully equipped gym and a separate two-bedroom apartment which Carlos and his wife Juanita occupied—this information supplied by Blake as the limousine rolled into the huge garage next to a black sports car and a white sedan.

'So what do you think?' he asked her.

'I think,' she replied, 'that you are a very lucky man to live in a house as amazing as this.'

'And *I* think,' Carlos added with a cheeky smile over his shoulder, 'that I am an even luckier man to have a boss like Señor Blake.'

Blake just laughed, but Kate could see he was pleased. Proud, too, of his house.

After meeting Juanita—who was as welcoming and cheerful as Carlos—Kate was given the grand tour by Blake. They started on the middle floor, which encompassed two large living areas, a bespoke kitchen, a home theatre, three en-suite guest bedrooms and another powder room for the use of guests, as well as a solar-heated pool which was entertainment heaven, with an indoor-outdoor barbecue and a cute cabana, complete with comfy lounge setting, a washroom and a built-in bar.

But it was the deck that led off the living area at the front of the house which took Kate's breath away.

'Oh, Blake,' she said, leaning against the wooden railing with a wondrous sigh. 'This is some view.'

That was an understatement. She could see for miles across the lightly timbered valley and over to the hill on which stood the famous HOLLY-WOOD sign.

'The view upstairs is better,' he said.

'Really?' She found that hard to believe.

'I'll show you. Then we'll come down and have

some dinner. Juanita's cooked something special for you. I knew you'd be too tired to go out.'

Kate actually didn't feel tired, despite not sleeping all that much on the plane. She'd been too excited. And too afraid. Not of flying. Or of Blake. But of what she had done, leaving her home and her country behind to be with Blake and pursue a career not on the stage, as she'd always intended, but in the movies—which was much more daunting to her.

Stage work was safe in Kate's eyes. Her looks weren't on display so much as they were in movies. She'd never been an overly confident or a bold person, but since meeting Blake she'd begun to change. He made her feel beautiful for starters. And now, tonight, in his company, she was changing again. No longer afraid, she felt both alive and confident. And, yes, free. Free of past failures. Free of her futile love for Lachlan. Free to really move on.

It was a delicious feeling.

'I hope you like chillies,' Blake said as he took her hand and led her up the thickly carpeted stairs to the top floor.

'I *love* chillies. I love all hot spicy food.'

'Good.'

The top floor was totally devoted to the master suite, consisting of the hugest bedroom Kate had ever seen, a bathroom which looked like a picture she'd once seen of a Roman bathhouse, and a spacious separate sitting-room-cum-study, complete with an enormous flat-screen TV on the wall.

But it was the wraparound deck which seduced and entranced Kate, with its view way beyond what she'd been picturing. She'd expected a better view of the Hollywood Hills, but when she walked round to the other side the city of Los Angeles lay before her, its many and colourful lights rivalling even those of Sydney on New Year's Eve. And beyond the city lay the ocean, dark and serene under the night sky.

'I don't know what to say,' Kate said, and smiled over at Blake. 'It's so gorgeous up here. Your whole home is splendid but, honestly, I could look at this view for ever.'

CHAPTER TWENTY

BLAKE HAD THE sudden urge to tell her that she could do that. All she had to do was marry him.

Crazy, really. Thank God he hadn't opened his mouth and said as much. Because he would have regretted it. And she would only have said no.

He told himself that it wasn't *love* compelling him to voice such idiocies. Just a temporary infatuation. And frustration. She was an enchanting creature and a highly desirable one. Give him a few weeks with her in his bed and he would come to his senses.

'So, are you going to stay with me in there?' he asked, nodding towards his bedroom.

Her eyes widened a little, but then she smiled. 'Do you want me to?'

'But of course.'

'I shouldn't…' she said, but her eyes were sparkling.

'But you will…'

'Of course.'

Of course, he thought ruefully as he swept her into his arms and kissed her, his head reminding him that she was still an actress even if she *was* different. And she was ambitious. If she hadn't been she wouldn't be here. Because she didn't love him. She probably still loved that idiot show pony, with his golden boy looks and sickeningly seductive charm.

His mouth worked hard to make her forget him—at least for now—and Blake didn't ease up until he felt her total surrender to the heat of the moment. She was a naturally sensual creature— he'd discovered that during the time they'd spent together in Sydney—and her celibacy over the past few years had made her ripe and ready for his attentions.

And attend her he would. Every day and every night. He would fill her body and her mind until she was incapable of wanting or even thinking of any other man. And he would spoil her rotten, seducing her with a lifestyle which few women would turn their backs on. And then, when the time was right, he just *might* ask her to marry him.

Okay, so it was still a crazy idea. But, crazy or not, the idea refused to be dismissed.

His mouth gentled on hers whilst his mind began working out how he could persuade her to throw her lot in with him. He reasoned that he could legitimately argue that marriage between people who liked and desired each other had a better chance of succeeding than those marriages entered into out of romantic love. He could point out that they would have a good life together. She would have *the* good life—a better one than her materialistic sister would have with lover-boy.

Blake suspected that getting one over Maddie would appeal to Kate. But his all-time winning argument might be that they didn't have to be married ''til death do us part'. If it didn't work out they could divorce, and Kate could walk away with a very nice settlement.

When love wasn't involved there would be no bitterness. And no children, of course. He would never expose a child to such a marriage.

Thinking about the 'no children' aspect forced Blake to accept that Kate would never go for such a proposal. The girl was a romantic of the first order. The best he could hope for was that she would agree to live with him. At least for now.

For some reason that eluded him Blake felt somewhat disgruntled with this solution to his current obsession with Kate. But it would have to do.

He lifted his head, satisfied to find that she was breathing heavily and her eyes were glazed.

'Sorry, sweetheart,' he said, and touched a tender fingertip to her softly swollen lips. 'As much as I would like to continue, Juanita will be upset if we let her food over-cook.'

Which was a lie, Juanita having informed Blake earlier in the day that their entrée and dessert were pre-prepared and cold, with a main course that would not take long to cook. But it was better than telling Kate the truth; that he was so hard for her he might not last if he went ahead and had sex with her right at this moment.

'Well, we can't have that, can we?' Kate said, her eyes clearing. 'She's much too nice to upset.'

Blake liked it that Kate liked his housekeeper. And Juanita seemed genuinely to like Kate back. She fussed over their meal, returning often to the table to see that everything was okay. Which it was. Juanita was a brilliant cook. Her guacamole was second to none, as were all her other Mexican and Spanish-inspired dishes.

Not that Blake ate at home all that often. He networked over lunches and dinners, both at fashionable restaurants and at the various golf clubs he frequented. When working in his office he often skipped lunch entirely, living only on coffee. Today he'd been too busy to eat much, so he was appreciative of the three-course meal—especially the seafood paella which was followed by his favourite dessert: fried ice-cream, which had a delicious coconut and cinnamon flavour.

Kate, he noted, ate everything as well—a lovely change from most women in Hollywood who hardly ate at all.

'If you keep feeding me gorgeous food like this, Juanita,' Kate complimented her over coffee, 'I'm going to put on weight.'

'You are not the type to get fat,' Juanita replied. 'Not like me.'

Juanita was an attractive woman, with wavy black hair and flashing brown eyes. She was, however, pleasantly plump.

'You are *not* fat,' Kate said.

Juanita smiled. 'And you are a lovely girl. Australians are very nice people, I think. Or most of them are. I am not so keen on that fair-haired actor who comes here sometimes. You know the one I mean, Blake?'

'Indeed I do.'

'He is rude to me. He has no respect.'

Blake frowned. 'I didn't know that. What does he say or do that's rude?'

She scowled. 'He is clever, that one. He waits until you are out of the room… It is not what he says so much. It is the way he looks at me—like I am beneath him because I am Mexican.'

Blake decided then and there that Lachlan would never enter his house again. Neither would he contract him for any more movies. It was time their relationship—such as it was—was at an end. And if at the back of his mind he knew this decision was all about Kate, he steadfastly ignored it.

'I'm sorry, Juanita,' he apologised. 'You won't have to put up with that ever again. He won't be back.'

'What do you mean?' Kate asked in shocked tones once Juanita was out of earshot.

Blake shrugged, then picked up his coffee cup.

'It's time Lachlan and I parted company. Aside from the lies he told you about me at the wedding, he's become too big for his boots. And, like *I* told you at the wedding, he's not that good an actor. He suits a certain type of part but he has no versatility. I want to move on from making romantic comedies. I have a hankering for some more serious movies—like the one I've offered you.'

'Do you think that's wise?' Kate asked, frowning. 'You made your name with those movies starring Lachlan. *The Boy from The Bush* has an enormous cult following.'

Blake tried not to react badly to her remarks, but found it impossible. 'Yes—silly female fans who think a handsome face, a good body and a dazzling smile is the be-all and end-all.'

He knew immediately that he had hurt her feelings. Her face told the story. Her face told him lots of stories—none of which he wanted to hear.

'I think you're wrong,' she defended, her cheeks flushing. 'Lachlan might not be Laurence Olivier, but he does have *some* talent. *And* star quality. I know he's vain and shallow, but I dare say lots of other movie stars are as well. Claudia Jay for one,' she added, with a curl of her top lip.

'True,' he conceded. 'Okay,' Blake went on, finding an apologetic smile with difficulty, 'he's not as bad as I'm making out. I'll admit that. But I don't like racists. Or philanderers.'

'Then perhaps you're in the wrong business,' Kate pointed out tartly. 'Hollywood is hardly renowned for treating minorities fairly. Or for its stars being faithful.'

Wow, Blake thought. *That's telling me.*

Kate might look and act quiet at times, but she knew how to voice an opinion. And, whilst it irked him that she might be defending Lachlan because she still had feelings for him, she was speaking a whole lot of truth.

His smile this time was full of admiration and respect. 'So you won't mind if I hire Lachlan for the occasional movie?' he asked, watching her closely to see how she would react.

'Why should I mind?' she shot back at him. 'If you think I'm still in love with the man, then you're dead wrong. I can see now that I was no better than those "silly female fans" you described. Who think "a handsome face, a good body and a dazzling smile is the be-all and end-all". I confess I used to watch his movies and drool with the rest of them. But I assure you I wouldn't drool now.'

Wouldn't you? Blake wasn't so sure about that. What was that saying about fearing a woman doth protest too much?

'I still won't be inviting him here to my home ever again. If and when we do business it will be at my office.'

'That's your prerogative, Blake. And your decision.'

Juanita coming in at that moment interrupted what was becoming an awkward conversation.

'More coffee?' she asked.

'No, thanks,' Kate said, and gave Juanita a warm smile.

Blake hadn't quite finished his yet, and said so.

Juanita nodded. 'Carlos wants to know what guest bedroom to put Kate's suitcase in.'

'None of them,' Blake told her. 'Tell him to put it up in my bedroom.'

Juanita smiled. *'Si,'* she said, and hurried out to tell her husband the news.

Kate glanced at Blake. 'Juanita seemed pleased.'

'She likes you.'

'Hasn't she liked any of your other women?'

'I have never had a woman stay here with me before—not even for a night.'

'Really? So where do you have sex, then? At their place?'

He had to laugh. It was a long time since he'd been with a girl who was so direct.

'Sometimes.' *And sometimes in trailers on location or in hotel rooms.* 'If you must know, my love-life has been very limited since I moved to America. In actual fact I hadn't had sex for several weeks before I met you.'

'*Really?* Why not?'

Why not, indeed? Maybe he was bored with the kind of women he'd been sleeping with. Maybe he was sick to death of one-night stands and ships that passed in the night.

Maybe I was waiting for someone like you, he wanted to say, but didn't. As a very experienced scriptwriter, he instinctively knew when something was too much too soon.

Blake shrugged. 'I'd been very busy working on Lachlan's last movie. It wasn't turning out as well as I would have liked. I needed to rewrite a couple of scenes and reshoot them. Then the editing afterwards was a nightmare. Most of it ended up on the cutting room floor. Thank God the movie's got a good score. Good music can do wonders. It won't lose money, but I doubt it will set the world on fire. Now, enough of this chit-chat, my love. I'll just finish up this coffee and then it's off to bed for us.'

CHAPTER TWENTY-ONE

'WHAT'S KEEPING YOU so long?' Blake called out to her from the bed.

Kate had insisted on having a shower first. *Alone*, this time—unlike when she and Blake had showered together during that sex-crazed night back in Sydney. She didn't want to do anything kinky with him. She just wanted to *be* with him, to have his arms around her and to have him make love to her as if she was really his love. It was silly of her, she knew, to feel like this about him. But she couldn't seem to help herself.

Was this true love at last? she wondered as she dried herself.

Her feelings were certainly different from what she'd felt for Lachlan. But she couldn't be sure yet. It was way too soon. But, oh, he made her so happy.

Kate smiled at this last thought. Because that

was what he'd said he wanted to make her. Happy. Well he'd succeeded all right. And how!

'If you don't get yourself out here pronto, madam,' Blake called out, 'I'm going to come in there and ravage you on the spot.'

'You are such a beast,' she said laughingly, and emerged from the bathroom demurely covered by a huge bath sheet.

'Take that damned thing off,' he demanded testily. 'Then get yourself in here.'

Kate liked it that she didn't feel nervous or shy with him, slowly unwrapping the towel and letting him feast his eyes on her naked body. She'd returned to the beauty salon the day before her flight was due and had every scrap of hair waxed off her body. And she meant *every* scrap.

Blake's eyes smouldered with desire as they raked over her. 'How did you know I like that look?' he said thickly.

'I didn't. I just hoped you would. And it makes me feel sexy.'

'You *are* sexy—with or without clothes.'

'You say the nicest things.'

'Not always.' And he threw back the bedclothes,

showing that he was not only naked but armed and ready for action.

She dived in and snuggled up to him, pretending to be shocked when he said what he wanted to do to her in rather crude terms.

'Such language,' she chided, and kissed him on the neck.

'Well, it's a much better word than *shagged.*'

'I agree with you. But I would prefer *make love*—do you mind?'

'Not at all. It's a lovely expression. Let's make love, then.'

'Yes, please.' And she lifted her face to his.

His kisses were gentle to begin with. But not for long. Kate welcomed the passion of his mouth. And his hands. Her breasts swelled in readiness for his caresses, her nipples aching to be played with. And play with them he did—sometimes tenderly, sometimes roughly. She gasped, then sighed, then gasped again.

'I love these,' he said, and pulled at them until they were even longer and harder.

When she thought she couldn't bear it any longer he moved on, one of his hands dipping down between her thighs to torture her there. But, oh, how she loved it. Loved it that he seemed to know exactly what to do. Loved it that he kissed her mouth at the same time…invading her in twin places.

He was a master magician with her body. But also with her head. For there were no bad thoughts to haunt her during his lovemaking. Nothing but the here and now, which was both blinding and blissful.

She cried out when he entered her at last, her body lifting to his, soaring higher and higher until it splintered apart. His name flew from her panting lips when she felt him come along with her. For what felt like ages she was suspended on a plateau of wild throbbing pleasure. And then she was falling, as though from a great height. But there was no fear…nothing but the sensation of freedom and, yes, love.

It was the last thought Kate had before sleep claimed her. That she loved this man who'd set her free—free to be the woman she'd always wanted to be.

Bloody hell, Blake thought as he held her sleeping body close. *If this isn't love then what is it?*

Whatever it was, it scared the living daylights out of him. Because it was almost out of his control. But only *almost*. He could still think, he supposed. Blake had always been of the belief that if he could still reason then he hadn't fallen into that particular honey trap. Not yet, anyway.

Easing her out of his arms, he withdrew, then practically staggered into the bathroom. His legs felt so weak. Yet he'd only had her once. Maybe it was the build-up of the last few days which had made his orgasm so momentous, so overwhelming. Or maybe it was just *her*. She did things to him—made him feel things and plan things which were quite alien to him.

Once he'd got over the fiasco with Claudia he'd lived a very independent lifestyle, not needing or wanting anyone in particular. He'd had the occasional girlfriend, but nothing serious. Sex for him had become nothing more than the scratching of an itch, so to speak.

Yes, his bed partners were still usually actresses, but that was only natural. In his line of work he met lots of actresses. They were invariably attractive girls, intelligent and amusing—and *very* keen to be seen with him. Sex with them was easy and satisfying, but instantly forgettable. He never made them promises he couldn't keep, never let them think there was any kind of future with him.

Blake hadn't lied to Kate when he'd said no other woman had stayed with him up here. After he'd moved into this house fifteen months ago he'd decided that it was going to be his private domain—a sanctuary where he could work and write and fantasise…not about sex, but about being lauded as the greatest movie-maker of the present day.

Success was very important to him. As it was to Kate, Blake reminded himself. He should never forget that. As wonderful as she was, she'd still had her eye on the main chance when she had accepted his offer of help plus his invitation to stay here at his house.

Yes, there was no doubt she found him attractive. Lots of women did. And, yes, she enjoyed sex with him. But she was still in the recovery phase after being in love with Lachlan. It would be foolish of him to imagine there was more to her feelings than gratitude and a whole heap of rebound lust.

Which was fine by him. He didn't really want her to fall in love with him, did he?

Did he?

Blake scowled as he flushed the toilet, washed his hands, then padded back to bed. She was still dead to the world, curled up in a foetal position under the quilt, cuddling her pillow as if it was her favourite teddy bear.

How young she looked. Young and vulnerable.

Be careful with her, Blake's conscience warned as he climbed into bed. *Don't hurt her. If you do you'll hate yourself. And you haven't hated yourself in quite a while.*

He didn't touch her again that night, despite his post-coital exhaustion quickly becoming a distant memory. He lay there next to her for ages, fiercely erect, before finally falling into a troubled sleep.

He woke before dawn and still he lay there, trying to relax—envying Kate, who hadn't moved a muscle. In the end, he rose, quietly pulled on a tracksuit and headed downstairs to the gym.

CHAPTER TWENTY-TWO

KATE WOKE SLOWLY, her eyes remaining closed whilst she wallowed in the warmth and comfort of the bed. It seemed *extra* comfortable this morning, she thought drowsily, wondering if her mother had put clean sheets on the previous day. Kate *loved* the feel of clean sheets…loved the—

Her eyelids shot up like a suddenly released blind. Kate sat up just as quickly, her rapidly clearing mind remembering everything in an instant. She was startled rather than shocked, because everything that had happened to her since she'd arrived in LA last night had been good. *Very* good. She regretted nothing. Absolutely nothing. Not even falling in love with Blake—who was, she'd already noted, no longer in bed with her.

Her eyes darted around the bedroom, which seemed even larger in the daylight, the curtainless windows and the sunshine having the effect of extending it out to the deck and the view beyond.

There was no sign of Blake anywhere. He wasn't in the bathroom—its door was wide open. So was the door to his study. Perhaps he was downstairs, having breakfast.

Kate's stomach growled, but it was her full bladder which demanded immediate attention. Jumping out of bed, she headed for the bathroom, sweeping up the discarded towel from the floor on the way, planning to use it as a cover until she could unpack and find the robe she'd brought with her.

No way did she want Blake returning to find her prancing around naked. She didn't mind being without clothes when he was making love to her—that seemed perfectly all right. But an exhibition-ist she wasn't. Or maybe she just didn't want to act like Maddie, who seemed to enjoy walking around in the nude—especially since she'd had her boob job.

Emerging from the bathroom with the towel wrapped around her, Kate went in search of her suitcase, which she knew was in one of the walk-in wardrobes. There were two. His and hers, pre-sumably. One was filled with Blake's clothes, the other empty, confirming Blake's claim that he'd never had a woman stay here before her—a thought which pleased Kate no end.

She wasn't under any illusion that Blake had somehow fallen in love with her. He didn't seem a 'falling in love' kind of man. But she was obviously special to him. And he obviously trusted her to let her stay with him in his bedroom. She could see that since his disastrous marriage he'd become somewhat of a cynical loner, using women just for sex and not letting any of them get too close.

Whilst she went about the business of unpacking, Kate wondered what it was about her exactly that he liked so much. It wasn't as though she was a great beauty. Or super-smart. Or highly experienced in the erotic arts. Though maybe that in itself held some kind of attraction. Maybe Blake fancied himself in the role of sexual tutor, getting off on showing her all the different forms of foreplay as well as many and varied positions for intercourse—most of which they hadn't tried yet, but all of which Kate had read about.

She was widely read, and her choice in books was quite eclectic, from biographies to historical sagas and lots of contemporary fiction, some of which included quite explicit sex scenes. She'd always known exactly why her limited sexual experiences in the past had been disappointing, and had once upon a time hoped that Lachlan would give her what she secretly craved.

That hadn't happened, of course. And, amazingly, she couldn't care less. He meant nothing to her any more. Her only regret was that she'd wasted four whole years believing he was the love of her life. The reality was that her feelings had probably been nothing but a youthful infatuation. Puppy love, spawned by Lachlan's golden-boy looks and his blistering charm.

When she thought about it in hindsight Kate felt somewhat foolish, though she consoled herself with the fact that most of the other girls at NIDA had fallen under his spell as well. None of *them* had seen him for what he was, either. But at the same time none of them had seemed all that heartbroken when he'd dated them, then dumped them.

Obviously they hadn't deluded themselves about his character as much as she had. Or maybe, once they'd spent time with him one-on-one, they'd seen the *real* Lachlan, not the good-looking charmer. Now that her rose-tinted glasses were well and truly off, Kate appreciated just how much he'd used her to help him with his acting. It had been cruel of him to take advantage of her like that. *Very* cruel.

Maddie was welcome to him, she decided. They were well matched, those two—both vain and selfish and horribly shallow. Not worth thinking about any more. Back to unpacking.

Kate retrieved her dressing gown and toilet bag, hurrying back into the bathroom to clean her teeth before hanging up the towel and then slipping into the robe. That done, she quickly brushed her hair, put it up into a topknot, then returned to finish her unpacking.

She hadn't brought a lot of clothes with her, only the things she really liked, as well as the new clothes she'd bought this week.

Kate smiled as she drew out her favourite new jacket. It was made of black velvet, which was very 'in' this year—or so she'd been told. It was cropped at the waist, with no lapels, and had silver zips decorating the pockets. Very stylish—and rather sexy when worn with her new tight white jeans and black high heels. The salesgirl had also talked her into adding a silvery grey silk cami, which she'd said made the outfit *'pop'*.

Kate couldn't wait to wear it all for Blake.

'And what are *you* smiling at, madam?'

Kate spun round at the sound of his voice. Blake stood in the open doorway, dressed in a navy tracksuit, a dark grey towel hanging around his neck.

Her smile was enigmatic. Or so she hoped. 'That's for me to know and you to find out.'

He grinned as he dabbed at his damp forehead with one end of the towel. 'I do love a mystery. *And* a challenge.'

She laughed. 'I don't think I've ever presented you with either. I've been putty in your hands from the first.'

His own smile was wry. 'You think?'

'I *know.*'

'You know nothing, sweetheart,' he said, in an enigmatic tone of his own. 'Now, I have to have a shower. I'm hot and sweaty. Have you show-ered yet?'

'No.'

'Good. Stop doing that for now, then, and have one with me.'

When she hesitated—she wasn't sure why— he raised his eyebrows at her. 'Come now, Kate, you're not going to start playing games with me, are you?'

She frowned, suddenly unsure of herself. It was one thing to fall in love with this man… Another thing entirely to let him think she would jump to his command *all* the time. It was tempting to say yes, but was that the kind of woman she really wanted to be?

Definitely not. But, oh, it was difficult to say no.

Her pride struggled to her rescue—though it had a fight on its hands. Because when he went all masterful like that she wanted to obey him… wanted to do whatever he wanted her to do.

'I'm not sure what sort of games you're referring to,' she said, with only the smallest quaver in her voice. 'I'm a very straightforward kind of girl. But I don't appreciate your ordering me into the shower like that. It's not…respectful.' Even as she said the word she thought how old-fashioned and prissy it sounded.

He stared at her for a long moment, then nodded. 'You're right. I apologise. It's just that you look so deliciously sexy in that silky thing you're almost wearing. Forgive me?'

Kate glanced down at her black and white robe,

which wasn't silk but polyester and had cost her all of fifteen dollars on sale. It was quite a modest garment, reaching past her knees, and it had three-quarter-length kimono-type sleeves. The sash belt, however, had come loose, and the neckline was gaping. But, since she didn't have much of a cleavage without a bra, she wouldn't have thought she looked at all sexy.

Kate yanked the lapels together and tightened the belt, aware that her nipples felt like bullets under her robe. 'Of course I forgive you,' she said, already regretting her stance. What was that she'd said about being putty in his hands?

'Would you *please* join me in the shower?' he asked politely, his dark eyes glittering with wicked intent.

She hadn't forgotten what he'd done to her the other night in Sydney when they'd showered together. The experience had been both thrilling and utterly seductive. She sighed, then shook her head at him, her own eyes glittering as well. She'd claimed she didn't play games, but this one was such fun. And wasn't that what he'd promised her from the start? That sex could be fun?

'I shouldn't,' she said. 'You will only take wicked advantage of me.'

'What if I promise not to, on the proviso that *you* take wicked advantage of *me*?'

Kate wasn't given to having lurid sexual fantasies, but her turned-on mind was suddenly filled with a clear image of how she could do just that. She could see herself now, taking a soapy sea sponge and slowly washing Blake all over. *All* over. She would order him to turn this way and that, so that not an inch of his body was unknown to her. Only one area would be neglected.

Kate would refuse to wash him *there* until he was going crazy with need…until his erection was hard and painful and, oh, so impatient, quivering wildly for her touch. Only then would she press the hot wet sponge around its base, squeezing it tightly and sliding it up and down. He would gasp at first, then groan, and finally he would come— right there in the shower. The violence of his release would send him lurching back against the wall, his outspread palms bracing himself against the wet tiles. His breathing would be ragged and his eyes glazed as they stared at her with shocked pleasure…

Of course it didn't quite work out that way. It started well, with Blake happy for her to wash his body, and amused at first when she bypassed his penis. But he was not a man to let *any* woman take control of things indefinitely.

'I thought you didn't play games?' he growled when she turned him around and began washing his buttocks.

'When in Rome…' she quipped, echoing what he'd said the previous night.

He sucked in breath sharply when she turned him around again and brushed the sponge across the tip of his swaying erection. His eyes darkened and his right hand shot out to grab her wrist, forcibly bringing the sponge to where he wanted it to be.

'You seem to have lost your sense of direction,' he said, his voice thick and his eyelids heavy.

Using his superior strength, he forced her to do at once what she'd planned to do eventually. But he stopped her before he came—stopped her and tossed the sponge away. Then he took her face in his hands and kissed her 'til she was lost in a haze of desire. It was Kate, then, who found herself pushed back against the wall, bracing herself whilst Blake sank to his knees before her.

'Oh, God,' she moaned when he spread her legs wide, because she knew how good he was at this. She had no hope of holding out—no hope at all. But she had to try. She didn't want to come like this.

So she lifted her eyes to the twin shower heads and watched the water gush out, trying not to think about how glorious it felt to have his lips and his fingers doing what they were doing, how her insides were twisting tighter and tighter, how she was already balancing on the edge of the abyss.

Her mouth had already fallen open in readiness for her release when Blake abruptly wrenched away from her and stood up.

'You can't stop now!' she cried out, her frustration acute.

He just smiled. 'Don't be greedy.'

He snapped off the water and bundled her out, grabbing a towel from a nearby rack and rubbing her roughly dry before doing the same to himself. Her hair was still dripping wet when he pulled her over to the double vanity unit and wrapped her hands over the edge, showing her flushed face reflected in the overhead mirror.

She could have protested…could have refused. But she did neither, just staying where he'd put her whilst he rummaged in one of the drawers and extracted a condom.

His entry was rough, but not painful—her body was supremely ready for ravaging—and their climaxes were simultaneous, their release more violent than ever.

He pulled her upright whilst their bodies were still shuddering together, holding her hard against him and nuzzling his mouth against her ear. 'God, Kate,' was all he said.

She didn't reply, her mind too dazed for her to make coherent conversation, her eyes tightly shut.

Never in her wildest dreams had Kate imagined sex could be like this. Because that was all it was that they'd just shared. It hadn't been making love. It had been just sex. Yet she'd thrilled to it all the same.

Her eyes opened and she stared at their reflection in the mirror, stared at his hands as they roved languidly over her breasts, down over her stomach, then between her legs.

'No,' she groaned when he started touching her in her most sensitive place.

He ignored her, and soon she gave up any hope of protest...

'You're very quiet,' he said to her over breakfast.

'I was just thinking,' she replied.

'About what?' He picked up his coffee and searched her face over the rim of the mug.

'About my screen test,' Kate lied. She'd actually been thinking that she wanted him again. 'When will I actually be doing it?'

'Probably Monday,' he said between sips. 'I'll organise an actor and a studio today.'

'I wish you didn't have to go to work,' she said, quite truthfully.

She would have loved to spend the whole day in bed with him. Or wherever he might want to have sex with her. The bathroom again. Or on the sofa in his study. She didn't care where. Kate suspected that if Juanita hadn't been hovering in the kitchen she might have tried to tempt him right here and now. She was only wearing her robe, nothing on underneath, and it was making her hotly aware of the moistness between her thighs.

She moved restlessly on the chair, desire squirming in her stomach. And lower…

Oh, Lord!

Love had turned her into a sex addict. Or maybe it wasn't love. Maybe it was just lust. Maybe she was deluding herself.

'Have to, I'm afraid,' he replied, putting his coffee down. 'I'm juggling several projects at the moment, all of which need my personal attention. Now, speaking of work, I'll need to get my lawyer on to your visa ASAP. I hope you were able to get everything I asked you to bring? Not just your references from NIDA, but the reviews of that play as well.'

Kate blinked at him, her mind having wandered to other things. Like how gorgeous he looked in that business suit. Gorgeous and sexy and…

'Kate?' he prompted, frowning at her.

'What? Oh, yes—yes. I got everything, and more. I remembered that the director of that play actually filmed our last dress rehearsal. I contacted him and he gave me a copy of the DVD.' She'd meant to tell Blake yesterday but she'd totally forgotten.

'That's fabulous. Because seeing is believing.

Much better than a letter just saying you're good. Something like that DVD could tip everything in your favour.'

'Only if my acting is good, though.'

'You know it is.'

She sighed. 'I thought so. But maybe people over here won't be impressed.'

'Now, don't start with that negative talk. Negative talk never gets you anywhere. Come on,' he went on, standing up. 'Let's go and get everything.'

After Blake had left Kate had another shower, then dressed in dark blue jeans and a lemon cotton top which suited her colouring and was not too warm, although the ducted air-conditioning was keeping all the rooms at a pleasant temperature.

It was only when she went out onto the deck or into the pool area that she felt cool. And then, not too cool. No doubt the day would warm up. There were no clouds in the blue sky. The weather reminded her of spring in Sydney.

Kate talked to Juanita for a while, offering to help her, but Juanita refused.

'No, no—you are a guest,' the housekeeper said. 'And you must be tired. Flying that far is very tiring. Or so I am told. I never fly anywhere. The thought terrifies me. Go and have a lie-down. Or watch a movie—Señor Blake has thousands.'

It was only then that Kate remembered Blake had left a printed copy of her script on the desk in his study upstairs, suggesting she read the whole thing through in order to fully understand the context of her part.

After getting herself another mug of coffee, Kate carried it upstairs and went into his study, settling herself onto a comfy leather sofa and placing her coffee on its built-in side table. She had just begun to read when the tell-tale ring of her phone infiltrated faintly, from where she'd left it on the bedside table.

Thinking it might be Blake, she hurried to answer it.

But it wasn't Blake.

It was Maddie.

CHAPTER TWENTY-THREE

'MADDIE!' KATE EXCLAIMED. 'What are you doing, ringing me? You're supposed to be on your honeymoon.'

'Honeymoon? *Huh*. Darling Lachlan spends more time on his phone than with me. His new American agent is negotiating some big movie deal for him. A franchise, apparently, all with the same hero. Rather like James Bond, only sexier. Not sure how it *could* be sexier... Anyway, he's very excited about it. Can't say *I* am. The money's fabulous, but all the films are going to be shot in Europe and he says I can't go on location with him. I'm supposed to stay home in Sydney like a good little wife.' She laughed. 'As if I'm going to do *that*. Anyway, that's not why I'm ringing you...'

Kate had an awful suspicion that she knew exactly why her sister was ringing her.

'I know all about your going to LA,' Maddie

rattled on. 'Mum told me everything. And I know you're staying in Blake Randall's house.'

'Yes...' It was only one word but it carried a whole heap of meaning. Such as *It's none of your damned business, Maddie.*

'Look, I'm not against what you've done. Hell, sis, I was all *for* it. Remember? But Lachlan's appalled. Lord knows why. I moved in with *him* the day after we met. Maybe things are different in America. Anyway, he wanted me to warn you about what people will soon be saying.'

'What people, exactly?'

'Hollywood people. Lachlan says they can be very small-minded and downright malicious. He said they'll be nice to your face but they'll snigger behind your back. They don't like unknowns like you getting the star treatment just because they're sleeping with the boss. He said you haven't paid your dues and that'll get right up their noses.'

'Well, thank you for the warning, Maddie,' Kate said, sounding much cooler than she was feeling. Why couldn't Maddie be *happy* for her? *She* had everything *she* wanted. 'But I don't much care what Lachlan says. As for my getting star treatment—Blake's only offered me a supporting part in this movie. It's not like I have the main role.'

'And you won't get one, either. Lachlan says he'll screw you 'til the movie's finished and then he'll toss you out on your ear. Lachlan says that…'

'I don't give a monkey's uncle what Lachlan says,' Kate bit out. 'He's just jealous. And possibly so are you.'

'That's not true!' Maddie denied. 'I'm just worried about you. I don't want you to get hurt.'

'Oh, really? Were those your sentiments when you honed in on the one man you knew I had a crush on?'

'I've already apologised for that.'

'At the same time admitting that you don't even love him,' Kate swept on angrily. 'You just want the good life, you said. Well, I'm having a better life now—with a man I *do* love,' she threw down the line without thinking. 'And you obviously don't like it one bit!'

Kate might have said more if Maddie hadn't hung up on her. She stared down into the silent phone, swamped by a mixture of frustration and fury. Finally she turned off the phone and threw the damned thing on the bed, determined never to speak to her sister again.

It was only when she sat down in Blake's study and picked up the script again that she realised her hands were shaking. No—her whole body was shaking.

It was then that she started to cry.

Blake tried Kate's phone again but it was still turned off. *Damn it*. She'd probably turned the darned thing off and gone back to bed for that rest he'd advised. Yet he really wanted to talk to her. Excitement was still fizzing through his veins.

What to do? He couldn't go home yet. He had a meeting with the head of Fortune Films this afternoon. To cancel at this late stage would not be wise. They were the only distribution company worth having, in his opinion.

Blake glanced at his Rolex. It was twenty past one. No way could he get home and back in time for the meeting at two-thirty. A light suddenly popped on in his brain, solving his problem. *Juanita*. He would ring her and have her go in search of Kate.

If she was asleep then it was high time she woke

up, otherwise she wouldn't sleep tonight. It was a thought which brought a wry smile to his face. Maybe he should let her stay asleep…

But, no, his news simply couldn't wait.

Kate was sitting out on the deck, dry-eyed, when Juanita found her a second time. She'd come up an hour ago, insisting Kate come down for some lunch. But Kate hadn't felt like eating, and had told Juanita she would be down a little later.

Now she was back, looking at Kate with concern in her dark eyes.

'Señor Blake has just rung me,' she said. 'He said he has been trying to ring you but your phone is turned off. He said he has good news and could you please ring him?'

Kate sighed, but did not move. She could not imagine any news which would make her feel better. It was silly of her to believe anything Maddie had said, but she was only human and doubts had crept in. Doubts about what she was doing. Doubts about Blake. Doubts about everything. On top of that, she hated it that Maddie had hung up on her—hated herself for trying to hurt her sister. Revenge was *not* good for the soul.

Juanita hovered. 'Señor Blake...' the house-keeper went on. 'He...he is a good man but not always a patient one. Please... He will think I did not give you the message if you don't ring him straight away.'

Kate heard the worry in Juanita's voice and immediately stood up. Juanita's relieved smile made Kate feel guilty. It wasn't like her to be so thoughtless.

'Sorry, Juanita. Please don't worry. I'll call him now.'

'That is good,' Juanita said, and bustled off.

Kate hurried into the bedroom and retrieved her phone and turned it on. Within a few seconds Blake was on the line.

'I hope I didn't wake you,' were his first words.

'No, no. I wasn't asleep. What's up?'

'I watched that DVD of your play and I have to tell you, Kate, I was more than impressed. You were *fantastic*. In fact I was so impressed I had a copy made and had it couriered over to the agent I think will suit you best. He promised to look at it this very afternoon and get back to me.'

'Oh,' she said, somehow unable to react normally, with her old friend depression having taken hold of her. 'That is good news.'

'You don't sound very enthusiastic.'

'Sorry. I think I might be a bit jet-lagged. I tried to read through that script, like you told me, but my eyes kept glazing over.'

'Then you really should try to get some sleep. I want to take you out to dinner tonight. To celebrate. Because there's no *way* they'll knock back your working visa once they see you in that play. You're a shoe-in, sweetheart.'

Kate couldn't tell him she didn't want to go anywhere. So she said nothing.

'Kate?' he said after a few moments' awkward silence. 'What is it? Something's wrong. I can tell.'

Kate sighed. 'Maddie rang me.'

Blake swore. 'And what did your darling sister say to upset you *this* time?'

Tears suddenly swam in Kate's eyes. 'It wasn't what *she* said so much. It was what Lachlan had told her to say.'

'About what?'

'About me coming to Hollywood with you.'

Blake swore again. 'That bastard needs sorting out. Tell me what he said. And I want to hear every single word.'

Kate swallowed the lump in her throat. Then she repeated every single word of Lachlan's warnings. But she didn't tell Blake what she'd said back to Maddie about loving him.

He didn't swear this time. He just listened.

'When I accused them both of being jealous,' Kate finished, 'Maddie hung up on me. That's why I turned off the phone. So she couldn't ring me back.'

'I see. And do you believe what Lachlan said about me this time?'

'No...'

'You don't sound so sure.'

'I... I thought he had a point saying that people will believe I'm sleeping my way to success. They *will* think that, Blake.'

His sigh was heavy. 'You can't spend your life worrying about what other people think.'

'I suppose not. It's just that I want to feel I'm succeeding as an actress through my own efforts.'

'That wasn't working so well for you when we first met, was it?'

'That's because I was not in a positive frame of

mind at the time. Maddie getting together with Lachlan had affected me badly. I coped whilst I was doing the play. It was the perfect escape from my melancholy, playing an upbeat girl who refused to let anything get her down. But when the play folded I lost what was left of my confidence. I was terrible at all my auditions. And I *looked* terrible. I can see that in hindsight. I wouldn't be terrible now. I *know* I wouldn't.'

'So are you saying you don't *want* this part in my movie?'

She hadn't thought that. Not until this moment. 'I think perhaps it's best I decline, Blake. I'm sorry. It was very generous of you to offer it to me, but…well…it just wouldn't feel right. Not now.'

'You mean since bloody Lachlan poisoned your mind about everything,' Blake snapped.

Kate could not deny that she'd begun having doubts about what she was doing here in Blake's house…what role she was playing. As much as she had enjoyed their interlude in the bathroom this morning, it had highlighted to her that Blake's feelings for her were probably largely sexual. His generosity and caring might not be real—just a means to an end. Falling in love with him might have blinded her to his true character.

'I wouldn't say "poisoned",' she said slowly. 'But he's given me food for thought.'

'You still love that bastard, don't you?'

'No,' she said truthfully. 'No, I don't. I told you that already.'

'I know what you *told* me, Kate.'

His scepticism shocked her.

'Love doesn't die that quickly,' he growled.

'It does when it wasn't true love in the first place.'

'If only I could believe that...'

Kate hated it that he didn't believe her. She ached to tell him that *he* was the one she truly loved, but she doubted he'd believe that, either. And if by some fluke he did, then it would just give him more power over her.

Not a good idea, Kate. She was having enough trouble sorting her head out as it was.

'I think it would be best if I went home, Blake,' she said shakily.

'No, it would *not*!' he roared down the phone. 'You hate it there.'

'I don't *hate* it.'

'Bull-dust. Your sister and your mother might not mean to, but they suck all the life out of you. Your family will make you feel like a failure if you go back now. And you're *not* a failure. You're a beautiful and talented actress who just hasn't had the right break yet.'

Blake's lovely compliments sent tears pricking at her eyes.

'You *have* to stay here, Kate. Okay, don't take the part I offered if it bothers you. Though damn it, girl, you're looking a gift horse in the mouth. I suppose that's why you don't want it? You think it's charity on my part, or something much worse. You don't realise just how fantastic an actress you are. I would *kill* to have someone like you in any of my movies. Hell, Kate, watching you in that play practically blew my mind.'

'But, Blake, you offered me that part *before* you saw me in the play,' she pointed out.

He was silent for a few fraught seconds, then he laughed. 'Okay, so you've caught me out. Yes, I wanted you, Kate—almost from the first moment I saw you—and I wasn't above using your ambition to get you into my bed. But I wasn't lying when I said I want to make you happy. I honestly do. You've touched something in me, Kate—something that is rarely ever touched. I'm not known for my empathy, or my compassion. And as for passion—the only passion I've had for years is for my movies. Until I met you. God, but I want you with *passion*, girl. And I need you. I won't let you go home—not whilst there's breath in my body. You're to stay here with me—not as a guest, but as my girlfriend. A proper live-in girlfriend. Then, once your visa comes through, you can knock yourself out going to endless auditions until you get yourself an acting job. And once you've made it on your own you will do a movie for *me*. Not some minor role but the lead, in a script I will write especially for you!'

Kate sucked in breath sharply. Lord, how did an aspiring actress in love say no to all *that*?

'And if you're worrying about how much money I'll have to spend on you until you're earning money on your own,' he charged on, 'then I'll keep a tally. You can pay me back as soon as you can. What do you say to that idea?'

'I'm pretty speechless right now.' *And brimming full of emotion.* Okay, so he hadn't said he loved her, but he did care about her. Passionately so.

'We can't let other people spoil what we have together, Kate. It's special—our connection, our chemistry. Don't you agree?'

'Yes…' she choked out.

'So you won't go home?'

'No.'

His sigh was a sound of total relief. 'Thank God.'

'But promise you won't try to change my mind about doing that part,' she said with a sudden rush of worry.

'I promise. It wasn't quite *you*, that role, anyway. You need to be the heroine of the story, not some slutty other woman. Now, I must get off this phone. I have an important meeting this afternoon. But I'll be home by six at the latest. If I'm going to be any later I'll ring you, so don't turn off your phone. And if your stupid sister rings you again *you* be the one to hang up.'

'I just might do that.'

'Good girl. I've booked dinner for us at seven. I won't be taking you to any of those celebrity restaurants—just a local steakhouse which does fabulous food. Wear something nice, but nothing over the top. The dress code at Jimmy's place is quite casual.'

'I've got just the thing.'

'Good. Have to go. Bye.'

He'd hung up by the time Kate said goodbye in return.

She sat for a long time, thinking about what he'd said. And what *she* had said.

She was proud of herself for deciding not to let Blake present her with her career on a silver platter. The temptation had been there to do just that. Face it, she'd been *well* on the way down that particular road. But, honestly, if she had she would never have felt good about any success which might have come her way.

Kate wasn't overly concerned about what perfect strangers thought of her, but she *did* care about what her family thought. Silly, really, but that was the way it was. Maybe one day she'd be able to be like Blake, not needing or caring about anyone back home. But that day hadn't come yet.

Kate already regretted being stroppy with Maddie over the phone. Maybe she should ring her back. Or text her.

And maybe not.

Best leave things for now.

Glancing at the time on her phone—it was after two—Kate decided to go in search of Juanita and that lunch she'd offered her. At the same time she aimed to find out where everything was in the main kitchen, so she could get herself her own breakfast and morning tea and lunch. She wasn't used to being waited on hand and foot and, whilst it was a deliciously pleasurable experience, Kate didn't want to become one of those spoiled rich women who wouldn't lift even one precious finger unless it was to get her nails done.

Not that she was *rich*. But she was living with a very rich man.

This was still the part which didn't sit well with Kate. Because it made her feel like a kept woman. A mistress. Being *any* man's mistress had not been in her life plan at all. Love did make a woman weak in some ways, but hopefully not in others.

Kate reaffirmed her determination to keep that tally Blake had mentioned, of what he spent on her. And to pay him back once she got herself an acting job. She also resolved to do some research on the internet, find out what was hot now in tele-

vision series. She knew that several young Australian actors had found work in LA that way.
Being unknown hadn't worked against them in
that field. It was, in fact, often seen as a plus. The
television industry loved new faces and fresh new
talent.

With these resolves fixed firmly in her mind,
Kate stood up, slipping her phone into the pocket
of her jeans before heading downstairs in search
of Juanita.

CHAPTER TWENTY-FOUR

'SORRY I'M A bit late!' Blake said as he dashed in shortly after six-thirty.

When Kate had heard him running up the stairs to the top floor she'd emerged from the bathroom, where she'd been titivating for the last half-hour.

He stopped to stare, his eyes turning hungry as they raked her over from top to toe. 'God, don't *you* look gorgeous?'

'Not too casual?' she asked as she hooked silver hoop earrings into her ears. Her hair was up in a loose knot, with a few wispy bits around her face.

'Not at all. I love girls in white jeans and heels. And I *love* that jacket.'

'So do I.' She flipped it open and shut, giving him a better look at the sexy silver cami, not to mention her braless breasts.

'Damn it, girl, you *really* make it hard on a man,' he growled, his dark eyes glittering. 'I desperately want to kiss you, but if I do we'll never get to the restaurant.'

Kate's heart started racing with a hunger of her own. 'Would that be such a disaster?'

'Not a disaster. But perhaps unwise. Because I'm starving. And starving is never good if a man wants to make love to his woman all night long.'

'All night long?' she choked out as her whole chest squeezed tight.

'Absolutely. Tomorrow's Sunday. I'm not going to work and I've cancelled my morning golf game. Which—and trust me on this—is not something I do very often. I love my golf. But I love making love to *you* even more.'

'Oh…'

His eyes narrowed on hers. 'You're not going to cry, are you?'

Kate swallowed, quickly pulling herself together. But that had been so close to him saying that he loved her. So heartstoppingly close…

'No, no. Absolutely not.'

'Good. Now, I'm going to have a quick shower. *Alone*. But I don't have time to shave or we'll be late. Do you mind me with a stubbly chin?'

'Not at all. It suits you. It's sexy.'

And it was. *Very.* It made him look like a pirate. Kate loved movies with pirates in them. Their characters were always masterful. And whilst they could be wicked, it was never in a horrible way. They just dared to do what a modern man wouldn't. Like kidnap women and then force them to fall in love with them…

A bit like what Blake had done to her.

Blake rubbed his chin. 'Sexy, eh?'

'Yes. *Very.*'

He laughed. 'You're not trying to seduce me, are you?'

'Could I?'

'*Could* you?' He shook his head at her, smiling a wry smile. 'Oh, that's funny, Kate. You've no idea how funny. Now, I suggest you go downstairs and have a pre-dinner drink. There's plenty of wine in the fridge. Or champagne, if you prefer. I won't be long.'

Blake slammed the bathroom door shut, sighing as he started reefing off his clothes. Lord, but she didn't know how close he'd come to reefing off *her* clothes—her very sexy clothes.

His plan to seduce Kate with sex was really backfiring on him. *He* was the one totally seduced and obsessed, and so in love with her that he could hardly contain the words.

I love you! he wanted to shout out. *I love you and I want to marry you!*

Once again the idea of marriage had jumped into his head, and it was beginning to annoy him. He didn't need to *marry* Kate just because he'd fallen in love with her. Why marry her? It was unnecessary in this day and age. They could just live together, as he'd already suggested, which would be so much easier, and much less complicated.

But it was no use. Marriage was what he wanted— along with her love. Nothing else would do.

'Stupid bastard!' he ground out, and stepped in under a cold shower, gasping as icy shards of water beat down on his overheated brain and body, bringing him back to reality with a rush. To a reality that was as sobering as it was sensible.

Because it was still way too soon to say such things to her. He *had* to give her more time. Had to let her get over that other stupid bastard before she was capable of falling in love with him.

Meanwhile he had to be patient. *Not* his favourite activity.

CHAPTER TWENTY-FIVE

JIMMY'S STEAK HOUSE was not a large establishment. Neither was it a place whose popularity rested on celebrity patronage, like lots of other Hollywood restaurants. Or so Blake told Kate on the way there.

'You'll like it,' he said. 'The food is great and it's quiet. There are no bands playing, nor even a piano player. They have booths as well as tables, so you can get some privacy, and you can actually hear yourself talk. I hate eating in places where you have to shout to be heard.'

Kate couldn't have agreed with him more.

'This is great,' she said, once they were seated in a booth well away from the door.

Of course she would think anywhere was great if she was with Blake. But she did genuinely like the quiet ambience and the decor, which was all clean lines and simple. White walls, wooden floor and tables, no tablecloths.

They hadn't been stared at when they'd come in, though all the ladies present had given Blake a few second glances. And why not? He looked devilishly handsome in black jeans, a white silk shirt—open at the neck—and a sleek lightweight black jacket. His casually sexy clothes, combined with his five o'clock shadow and his slightly rumpled black hair, gave him that bad-boy image women found so attractive.

Kate was no exception.

'Do you like red wine?' he asked as he picked up the drinks menu.

'It's okay,' she replied. 'But I prefer white.'

'You can't drink white wine with steak,' he pronounced, with his usual arrogance.

He ordered red wine, and Kate discovered to her surprise that she did like it. Or at least she liked this particular red wine, which she suspected was hideously expensive. It had a French label, and the waiter treated the bottle as if it was made of gold.

'Well?' Blake asked after she'd had a few sips.

'Lovely,' she replied.

'I told you so. You *must* widen your horizons, Kate.'

She smiled. 'I've widened them quite enough already, don't you think?'

He frowned. 'What do you mean?'

'You *know* what I mean.'

'I suppose you're referring to throwing in your lot with me?'

'Yes. I suppose I am.'

'Best thing you ever did. You were losing your way back in Sydney.'

Kate sighed. 'Don't you *ever* have doubts, Blake?'

He looked at her hard, then laughed. 'Everyone has doubts, Kate. But you have to learn to ignore them and just go for what you want. Otherwise you'll spend your whole life regretting your lack of courage.'

'Is that what you've always done? Just gone for what you wanted?'

'In the main. I was seriously derailed once—but you don't need to hear about that.'

Kate presumed he was referring to his divorce. *Horrid* thing, divorce. Especially if there were children involved...

'How long did it take for you to get back on the rails?' she asked him.

'How long?' he mused, lifting his glass to his lips for a long sip. 'Not too long. But I was terribly bitter for a while. Which I now regret. Bitterness is as self-destructive as revenge. And it gets you nowhere. You have to learn to move on and not dwell on the past.'

'You're talking about Claudia, aren't you?'

'Partly.'

'What do you mean by that?'

'I was talking in general—not just about Claudia in particular. I harbour no animosity towards Claudia any more. I met her the other week at a party and we had quite a pleasant chat. She's not too bad when you're not in love with her.'

Kate hated to think that he'd *ever* been in love with her. Which was pathetic, really.

Their steaks arrived at that fortuitous moment—Blake's medium rare and hers well done. Both were accompanied by French fries and salad, plus a side dish of herbed bread. The steaks covered half the plate.

'My goodness,' she said. 'I wish you had a dog. Then I could take him home some of this steak. I'll never eat it all.'

'You might have done, if you'd had it medium rare like me. Goes down much easier that way.'

'No, thanks,' she said, crinkling her nose at him. 'I don't like eating meat with blood in it.'

'Have you ever tried it?'

'No...'

'Then don't knock it 'til you try it.'

'Okay. Give me a mouthful of yours, then.'

He did—and she did like it. It was very tender... more tender than hers.

'See?' he said smugly. 'You shouldn't be afraid to try new things, Kate.'

'Yes, boss.'

He laughed. 'You sounded just like Carlos, then.'

'And *you* sounded like an old schoolteacher of mine. Not one I overly liked.'

'*Ouch*. That's not good.'

'No—so cut it out with the life lessons. I'll get there, Blake. In my own good time.'

He cocked his head to one side. 'You've become quite an independent little miss during the past week, haven't you?'

'I hope so.'

'Good. I like that. Now, eat up or the food will get cold. Nothing worse than cold steak.'

They both tucked in, and Kate realised how hungry she actually was. She ate ninety percent of the steak and all of everything else—including the herb bread.

'I like to see a girl with a good appetite,' Blake said as he dabbed his mouth with a serviette. 'Rare thing in Hollywood, I can tell you.'

'I'm lucky that I can eat whatever I like and not get fat. I have a fast metabolism.'

'That *is* lucky. And good for your career. You'll stay slim and at the same time you won't get all skinny and fragile like some of the actresses I know. Speaking of your career... I was talking to Steve late this afternoon and—'

'Who's Steve?'

'Steve Kepell. The agent I think would suit you. The one I sent the DVD of your play. Anyway, he was as impressed as I was—both by your acting and your looks. Said you were very photogenic. But he *did* suggest that whilst you're waiting for your working visa to come through you have some lessons from a dialect coach. Get rid of your Australian accent entirely. Oh, and he also suggested you have a few sessions with an audition coach. He gave me the name of a good one. Anyway, I'll line up both for you on Monday so that you can get started ASAP.'

Dismay swamped Kate, and her forehead bunched up into a troubled frown.

'What?' he asked.

She shook her head at him. 'I'm sorry, Blake, but it's all getting a bit too much.'

'What is?'

'Everything you're doing for me.'

He sighed. 'You're not going to say no again, are you?'

'Coaches like that are very expensive. I'm not dumb. I know what they cost.'

'But I can afford it,' he told her, her voice tight with obvious frustration. 'My movies are raking in heaps.'

'That's not the point. People will say I'm a freeloader, or a gold-digger. I know you said I shouldn't worry about what other people think, but I do.'

Blake scowled. 'They wouldn't say either of those things if you were my wife.'

'Your *wife*?' Kate exclaimed.

CHAPTER TWENTY-SIX

BLAKE COULD HAVE cut his tongue out. He'd done it now, hadn't he? But, damn it all, he was beginning to see everything he wanted getting away from him. And he couldn't bear it.

The shock on Kate's face just about killed him. Clearly marrying him was the last thing she wanted, or would ever do. And whilst one part of him found pleasure in this undeniable proof that she was nothing like Claudia, the rest of him was plunged into the most alien despair.

True to his nature, however, Blake refused to admit defeat. With a will of iron he climbed out of the pit and put his intelligence to finding the right words to say to her, finally adopting what he hoped was the right expression. One of mild exasperation.

'Yes, yes,' he said, with a flourish of his left hand, 'I know exactly what you're going to say.

We've only known each other a week. You don't marry someone you've only known for a week.'

'I… I wasn't going to say any of that at all,' Kate denied, feeling both flushed and flustered.

Because of course she would marry him in a heartbeat if he loved her. The brevity of their relationship didn't matter. She already knew more about him in a week than she'd learnt about Lachlan in four years. Kate knew down deep that Blake was a decent man. Caring and kind and above all fantastically good in bed.

'I was going to *say*,' she went on, having to force out the words, 'that I would only marry you if we were both madly in love with each other.' Blake's not loving her was a deal-breaker. Kate needed her husband to love her. 'I'm sorry, Blake, but marriage without love is not for me.'

'I see,' Blake bit out. 'Well, that's it then.' He looked at her for a long moment, his dark eyes searching hers as the corner of his mouth lifted in a strange smile. 'You wouldn't consider it even if one half of the couple was madly in love with the other?'

The truth behind his statement hit Kate with a squall of anxiety and embarrassment. 'Oh, no!'

she wailed, her stomach churning. 'You rang Lachlan, didn't you? And he *told* you. Or Maddie told you. I *knew* I should never have told her. Oh, God...'

And she buried her face in her hands momentarily, before looking up at him again with anguished eyes.

Blake shook his head at her. 'Kate, I don't know what in hell you're talking about. I haven't rung Lachlan. Though I will. Soon. He needs to be sorted out. But I haven't yet. And I certainly haven't talked to your sister.'

Kate blinked in confusion, then blinked again—until suddenly she realised what this meant. If he hadn't talked to Maddie or Lachlan then he didn't *know* she loved him. So he had to have been talking about himself.

Her heart flipped right over at the enormity of her discovery.

'Are you saying that you're actually in *love* with me?'

His smile carried amusement. 'Not "actually" so much as madly. Yes, Kate, my sweet. I'm madly in love with you. Is that so surprising? Now, what on earth were you going on about just now? What was it you told Maddie that she shouldn't have told me even though she didn't?'

'Oh. Yes. Oh. No. Oh. Well…' God, she was babbling like an idiot.

'Out with it, woman. No lies, now.'

'I… I told her that I love you.'

Blake seemed stunned. 'You *love* me?'

'Yes. Yes, I love you. Very much.'

'Wow… I never dreamt…' His hands lifted to run rather shakily through his hair. His gaze searched her face with an air of wonder. 'I thought it was too soon. I thought…'

'I know what you thought, but you were wrong. Lachlan means no more to me now than Claudia does to you. The moment you came into my life I saw that he was just a cardboard cut-out hero, whereas you are the real thing.'

'I'll have to remember to use that line in one of my movies.'

'You will not!' she said. But she was smiling.

'Right. Now, can we go back to that earlier part of our conversation where I suggested you become my wife?'

'Oh, *that* part.'

'Well, what do you say?'

The temptation to just say yes was acute. But…

'You need to ask me properly first—with an engagement ring in your pocket. And the wedding won't be taking place until after I get my first independent acting job, gained by my own efforts and no help from you.'

'Done!' he agreed, grinning as he whipped out his phone.

'What are you doing?' Kate asked breathlessly. She was still in a bit of shock at the speed of everything.

'I'm calling Carlos.'

'Yes, boss?' Carlos answered. 'You ready to be picked up?'

'Yep. But we won't be going straight home. I need to do some shopping first. Oh, and bring Juanita with you.'

'Juanita?'

'Yep. I know how much your wife likes jewellery. She'll know exactly where we should go to buy an engagement ring.'

'I'm sure she will,' Carlos replied gleefully. 'See you outside in about ten minutes, boss.'

'Perfect.'

CHAPTER TWENTY-SEVEN

BLAKE LAY BACK in bed with his fiancée in his arms, feeling happier than he could ever have imagined. His original quest to make Kate happy had been achieved—she hadn't stopped smiling or admiring her engagement ring for the last hour—but his own happiness exceeded anything he'd ever experienced before.

Who would have believed that an old cynic like him could find true love—and with an actress, no less? It was the ultimate irony. But a logical one in a way. Who else would he have so much in common with? Who else would understand him the way Kate did?

Byron was going to be surprised. Or perhaps not. Since marrying Cleo and becoming a father Byron had become an old softie. He would rejoice in their news and give Blake his heartiest congratulations and best wishes. Blake vowed to ring and tell him in the morning.

He wouldn't, however, be ringing Lachlan. If the rumour mill was correct he'd soon be severing his connections with Fantasy Productions anyway. Blake didn't bother to hope that Lachlan's new venture would fail because it probably wouldn't. Action heroes didn't have to be great actors. Blake didn't really care either way, but he vowed not to have anything more to do with the man—either personally or professionally.

'Will you stop admiring that damned ring?' he said now, pretending to be angry, 'and give your new fiancé some much-needed attention.'

'Rubbish. You've had plenty of attention. I still can't believe we're engaged.' And she wiggled her left hand back and forth, the five-carat brilliant-cut solitaire diamond glittering under the light of the bedside lamp.

'Well, Carlos and Juanita believe it. They wanted to throw us a party tomorrow night, but I said no because Sunday is their day off. Instead I'm going to take my wife-to-be out for the day. I've booked lunch for us at the Polo Lounge at the Beverly Hills Hotel, and then we're going to drive down to my favourite country club and I'm going to start teaching you how to play golf.'

Kate grimaced. 'That'll be a disaster. I'm not very sporty, you know.'

'With *your* build? You'll be a natural.'

And, surprisingly, she was.

Kate smiled during the whole drive home. They hadn't gone in the limousine, instead taking Blake's Porsche.

'I *was* good, wasn't I?' Kate said smugly as they walked hand in hand up the steps into the house.

'You sure were. *Too* good. In no time you'll be beating me. Well, perhaps not. But you could probably beat Byron.'

'Darling Byron. He seemed genuinely happy for us over the phone, didn't he? And not at all shocked.'

'Men like Byron never get shocked. Not like mothers.'

Kate was taken aback. 'You told your *mother*?'

'Hell, no. That can wait until after we're safely married. Same with yours. Then they can't spoil anything, can they? Not once we're a *fait accompli.*'

Kate flashed him a questioning glance. 'How long do you think it will take me to get a job?'

'No time at all once your visa comes through.'

'I can't wait.'

'We don't *have* to wait, you know. We could fill in the marriage licence form online tonight and be in Vegas for a wedding tomorrow. What do you say?'

Kate shook her head. 'No. Let's not be silly. Let's wait. Do you want coffee?'

'Yes, but I need to go to the bathroom first. Be back in a jiff.'

Kate put on the coffee machine. after which she toddled off to the nearby guest powder room. When she returned to the kitchen Blake was there, humming as he took down two mugs.

'You know, I rather like the idea of a Vegas wedding,' Kate told him. 'Provided I have a proper wedding dress and you wear a tux. We have to have decent photos to show our children.'

'Children!' Blake exclaimed, having not thought of their having children until that moment.

'Well, of course. Don't you *want* children?'

Blake considered the idea, and then decided he did. Kate would make a wonderful mother. He wasn't so sure about his own fathering capabilities, but he would give it his best shot—like he did with everything he attempted in life.

'Yes, I'd like children. Though I don't want a big family. Two would be enough. Though perhaps one would be better,' he added drily. 'No sibling rivalry then.'

'True. Okay, we'll settle on one until we see how the land lies. Of course I have to warn you that I might change my mind and eventually want six.'

Blake laughed, then turned and drew her into his arms. 'That's a woman's privilege, I guess. Though you're not to change your mind about marrying me.'

'As if I would.'

'Tell me again that you love me,' Blake urged, and pulled her even closer.

'I love you, Blake Randall,' she said, her eyes going smoky.

'And I love *you*, Kate Holiday.'

'Perhaps you should show me how much,' she suggested saucily.

'What about the coffee?'

'It isn't going anywhere.'

Blake smiled, then bent his mouth to hers.

EPILOGUE

Four and a half years later...

KATE SAT AT her dressing table, putting the finishing touches to her make-up and doing her best to keep her nerves under control. Tonight was a big night for her. And for Blake. It was the premiere of the movie Blake had once promised to write especially for her—a romantic drama, with Kate as the heroine and not a nasty line in the whole script.

Which had come as a huge relief!

Up until now Kate hadn't done any movies at all, concentrating on the television series which had been the first job offered to her, and which had gone on to be a huge success. She had already done several seasons, with more to come.

It was part of what was called the *domestic noir* genre, and Kate's character was a black widow type who was wickedly amoral, going through a new husband each season—one murdered, one dead of natural causes and the rest divorced—whilst having countless affairs on the side.

According to the producer, she'd been chosen for the part for two reasons. She was a total unknown and she didn't look the *femme fatale* type, which added an ironic edge to her actions and made her character compellingly fascinating to watch, making the audience wonder *What next?* all the time.

Of course her character—Amanda—only ever married rich men, and she was always dressed to kill. And when Kate had fallen pregnant for real, towards the end of the first season, the writers had just written a pregnancy into the second season—though of course they'd made sure Amanda's new husband wasn't the father. More drama that way.

The show was called *The Career Wife*, and it had already won several awards.

'When can I start wearing make-up, Mummy?'

Kate smiled at her daughter in the dressing table mirror. Charlotte—already nicknamed Charlie by Blake—was lying face down on the nearby bed, with her pretty face propped in cupped hands. She'd only turned three a few months ago, yet she seemed so much older. Though thankfully not too spoiled. Her English nanny had seen to that. And so had Juanita, who loved Charlotte dearly but refused to let her act like some pampered princess.

'Not just yet, darling,' Kate said gently. 'Perhaps when you're—'

'Eighteen,' Blake said firmly as he emerged from the bathroom, looking very suave in his black tuxedo.

'Eighteen?' Charlie squealed, sitting up and scowling at her father. 'Oh, Daddy, don't be so silly. I think seven is a good age—don't you, Mummy?'

'Er...' Kate didn't know what to say.

'Over my dead body,' Blake growled. 'Thirteen, my girl. And that's my final word!'

Kate smiled, noting how smug their daughter was looking, though she tried to hide it.

She even came up with a sulky pout. 'You *are* a meanie sometimes, Daddy.' But, having said that, she added sweetly, 'But a very *handsome* meanie.'

He laughed. 'Oh, go on—get out of here, you little minx. Your mother and I have things to talk about.'

Charlotte scrambled off the bed and ran out of the room.

'You *do* look handsome,' Kate said as she stood up and headed for her walk-in wardrobe.

Blake's hand shot out to grab her as she walked by, spinning her round into his arms.

'No, don't!' Kate squawked before he could kiss her. 'You'll ruin my make-up.'

'Bloody make-up,' he grumbled, but let her go. 'Wait 'til I get you home later,' he threw after her.

She smiled over her shoulder. 'Promises, promises...'

Kate was still smiling as she reached for her outfit. It wasn't a typical glamorous gown of the kind that most actresses wore to premieres and award nights. It was much simpler. Some would say conservative. It was a long cream crêpe skirt with a matching jacket, nipped in at the waist and then reaching down past her hips, giving her slim figure an hourglass shape. But Kate did add a touch of Hollywood glamour with a star-shaped diamond brooch and matching drop earrings, shown to advantage with her hair elegantly up.

'You look utterly gorgeous,' Blake said. 'I love that outfit. Where did you get it?'

'I had it made especially. I didn't want to wear

anything like I wear on my TV show. I wanted to look classier than that.'

'Well, you certainly do. But sexy at the same time. Sometimes less is more.'

'No more compliments or I might let you kiss me.'

When he came forward with that look in his eyes she laughingly warded him off, snatched up her clutch purse and hurried towards the door.

Blake sighed and hurried after her.

'Thank you so much for minding Charlie for us tonight, Juanita,' Kate said.

Blake had give Charlotte's nanny two tickets to the premiere, and she was coming with a fellow nanny whom she'd met in a local park and who had become her best friend. Juanita and Carlos had already seen the movie, at an early screening which Blake had organised to get audience reaction. They'd loved it—and so had everyone else.

Kate still felt horribly nervous, her mouth dry and her heart racing. It was her first movie, after all. And what made her even more nervous was the fact that her parents and Blake's parents were going to be there, Blake having generously paid for the four of them to stay for a few nights in one of the hideously expensive bungalows at the Beverly Hills Hotel, only a short walk from the theatre.

'Money well spent,' he'd declared when she'd protested at the expense. 'You don't honestly think I'm going to have them all staying *here*, do you? Heaven forbid!' And he'd literally shuddered.

Both sets of parents had eventually come to terms with Blake and Kate eloping to Vegas, but none of them had exactly been happy at the time. Kate could still remember the dire warnings which had come from her mother.

'It won't last, you know. Still, I suppose you can always get a divorce and come home...'

Blake's parents had been equally negative in their prognostications.

'Not *another* actress, Blake. Oh, dear. Some people just don't learn.'

The arrival of Charlotte a little over a year later had certainly helped smooth things over—as had both Kate and Blake's ongoing success. And a visit home to Sydney last Christmas had been a big hit. Charlotte had been at her adorable best and no one had been able to resist her charm.

Even Maddie had fallen in love with her—dear,

irrepressible Maddie, whose marriage to Lachlan had ended two years ago after Lachlan had been widely reported on social media as having affairs with every single one of his leading ladies. Though pretending to be heartbroken at the time, Maddie had happily taken a huge settlement—along with the house in Sydney they'd bought together—and promptly got back with Riley the plumber.

Leopards really didn't change their spots, did they?

Lachlan certainly hadn't. But his comeuppance was on the horizon. His career had faltered after his last movie, which had had some not too stellar reviews.

The movie business was a risky business—Kate knew that. And an actor's popularity could disappear overnight.

Such thinking sent a nervous shiver down her spine, made her hands twist together.

'Everything is going to be fine,' Juanita said, and clasped Kate's trembling hands in both of hers. 'You are a great actress. That is a great movie.'

Carlos said much the same on their way to the

theatre. But the kind words didn't lessen Kate's escalating anxiety. They were friends, after all. And all those other people who'd come to the pre-screening had been fans of Blake's work. They might not have wanted to tell him the truth: that the movie wasn't great and Kate was simply awful as a romantic heroine as opposed to playing the conniving villain she played in *The Career Wife*!

'Are you all right?' Blake asked her as they pulled up outside the theatre.

Huge crowds had gathered on the sidewalk, along with lots of paparazzi.

Kate refused to load her anxiety onto Blake. No doubt he was feeling a little tense himself.

'No, no. I'm fine,' she said.

'Good—because there's nothing to be nervous about. Byron rang me while you were getting ready. He and Cleo had just watched the copy of the movie I sent him and they were over the moon about it. Said it was going to make us all a small fortune. The only reason they aren't here in person to celebrate is because their son is due in two weeks' time.'

'Yes, I know. But let's not forget Byron and Cleo are biased. They're friends.'

'And very canny investors. Byron doesn't wear blinkers when it comes to money. Trust me when I say you're about to become an even bigger star than you already are.'

'Promise?'

'That's not a promise. That's a fact.' And he leant over and kissed her on the cheek.

Kate's anxiety eased slightly at his confidence, and his love. Somehow she found a smiling face for the photographers, but didn't linger in the foyer, hurrying into the theatre, where she smiled some more at the already seated guests before thankfully sinking into her own seat.

Finally, after considerable delays and endless advertisements, the movie started—by which time Kate thought she was going to be sick. She tried to concentrate but her focus seemed blurred. Suddenly all she cared about was what the audience was feeling and thinking. She had to force herself not to look around and stare at people's faces.

She did sneak a few surreptitious glances at her parents, who were sitting on her left. They seemed wrapped up in the drama, and her mother's mouth was slightly agape. Was that a good sign or a bad sign?

Finally, after what felt like an eternity, the movie ended and the credits started rolling. For a few seconds there was a deathly silence. Kate didn't know what to think. And then, as one, everyone in that theatre stood up and started clapping. Clapping and shouting *Bravo!*

Even Blake seemed surprised. And touched—especially at the sight of his dad, clapping the loudest.

Kate was just stunned, and her eyes filled with tears when her mother turned to her and said, 'Oh, my dear. You were just wonderful. I'm so, *so* proud of you.'

Kate and Blake stood up to more cheers, and Kate turned to the man she knew was responsible for this moment—the man responsible for every happy moment in her life.

Reaching up, she kissed him softly on the mouth and whispered, 'Thank you, my darling. For everything.'

Blake's dark eyes were full of love and admiration as he took her hand and lifted it to his lips. 'No,' he murmured. 'Thank *you*.'

* * * * *

LET'S TALK
Romance

For exclusive extracts, competitions
and special offers, find us online:

f facebook.com/millsandboon

⊙ @millsandboonuk

🐦 @millsandboon

Or get in touch on 0844 844 1351*

For all the latest titles coming soon,
visit millsandboon.co.uk/nextmonth

*Calls cost 7p per minute plus your phone company's price per
minute access charge

Want even more
ROMANCE?

Join our bookclub today!

'Mills & Boon books, the perfect way to escape for an hour or so.'

Miss W. Dyer

'Excellent service, promptly delivered and very good subscription choices.'

Miss A. Pearson

'You get fantastic special offers and the chance to get books before they hit the shops'

Mrs V. Hall

Visit millsandbook.co.uk/Bookclub and save on brand new books.

MILLS & BOON